Reunion of the Undead

My Life Among the Undead:

Book 6

Camara M. Bragdon

My Life Among the Undead Books

By

Camara M. Bragdon

Friend of the Undead

Yard Sale of the Undead

Secrets of the Undead

Carnival of the Undead

Holiday of the Undead

DEDICATION

This book is dedicated to all my fans. Thank you for all your encouragement and support.

CONTENTS

Chapter One:

I Get More than Just Birthday Presents

It was a crisp January evening in the city-state of Zephyr, but I didn't mind because I was helping my dad and my stepmother decorate for my birthday party. None of the guests had arrived yet, but it was still early. "Shelly! Amelia!" my dad called from the kitchen. "We're all out of milk! I'm going to run to the store." The tall, muscular former police officer stretched out his arm and goosed Amelia Anderson before heading out the door. "Need anything?"

My stepmom, a pretty woman in her fifties, gave him a horrified, but amused look. "Timothy Michael Anderson, not in front of your daughter!"

"Shelly's twenty-six, Amelia and I think she can handle it," he reminded her as he shut the door behind him.

Amelia shook her head at my father and continued to set the festive green and pink paper plates on the long oak table. Amelia and Dad had been happily married for a little over a month.

"I think Dad's using his superpower for bad," I told her with a smile.

Okay, maybe you're a little confused right now. So, let me explain some things. My name is Shelly Anderson. I'm a librarian in Zephyr. This magical city-state and others like it are your mythological melting pot. You've got every kind of fantasy creature you can imagine living here. My family has been in Zephyr for about six years. Dad, Amelia, my older brother, Robin, and I came into Zephyr from a dull, non-magical world. Human beings, like myself, acquire a magical ability when they come through a magical portal. My dad can stretch his body into any shape without hurting himself. This can gross people out. His wife, Amelia, is telekinetic. Robin, a cop on the Zephyr police force, can control plants with his mind.

My magical talent is telepathic communication. People might think this is a superb magical ability, and I'm somewhere up there with Professor X and Martian Manhunter. I'm pretty sure they could communicate telepathically with everyone, not just four races of people. Yep, four races: vampires, werepeople, ghosts, and zombies. I have telepathic communication with the undead.

I inherited my deep blue eyes from my father and straight, brown hair is a gift from my deceased mother. I'm just your average telepathic librarian. Of course, my fiancé would say I'm the hottest woman he's ever been with.

I was beginning to fold the pink paper napkins when I heard the familiar sound of a motorcycle pulling into the driveway. I dropped everything I was doing and sprinted to the front door. "Eddie's here!" I called behind me as I bounded out the door to greet him.

The very handsome Eddie Van Helsing was just turning off his green motorcycle. He took off his helmet, revealing a head full of short, curly, black hair. "Well, it's not every day I get a greeting like this," he told me as he climbed off the motorcycle. He kissed me on the lips before opening up the box on the back of the bike. "Are you going to do this every day when we get married?"

"Only if you bring me presents," I said as I watched my vampire open up the box. There were two wrapped presents and a bouquet of purple and white striped roses, all no bigger than the palm of my hand. "Oh, good, teeny weeny presents and flowers."

Eddie rolled his dashing green eyes at me as he put the items in his hand. He waved his free hand over the presents and the flowers, speaking the magic spell. "Maximum five." The presents grew to their normal size. He handed me the flowers. "Happy birthday, babe," he said.

I inhaled the heavenly scent of my favorite roses. "Good choice, hon," I told him as we walked into the house.

Amelia was standing by the stove, stirring a pot of pasta. "What lovely flowers, Shelly," she said the moment her hazel eyes spotted my gift.

I put my free arm around Eddie's waist. "Isn't he great? They're my favorite flowers," I told Amelia.

She retrieved a green glass vase from one of the oak china cabinets and filled it halfway with water from the kitchen sink. Taking the flowers from me, she placed them in the vase. Then she used her mind to set the vase on the counter facing the front door.

"Do you need any help, Mrs. Anderson?" Eddie asked as he balanced my presents in his arms. A jewelry box-sized present teetered on the edge of the larger present.

"I'll take that, Eddie," I volunteered as I took the presents from my fiancé. Running my finger along the edge of the biggest present, I felt a breach in the wrapping and began to gently open it.

"Shelly!" Eddie's voice echoed from the kitchen. "Don't even think about opening your present!" Drat, his heightened hearing!

I quickly set the boxes down on the official gift table. "I'm not doing anything."

He came into the dining room carrying a big bowl of pasta primavera. He raised an eyebrow at me as he set the food on the table. "Right? Why do I have a hard time believing you?"

"Because you should always believe the birthday girl who happens to be your fiancée." I glanced wistfully back at Eddie's perfectly wrapped presents. Something was stuck under the light green envelope taped to the largest present. I gently removed it. It was a very elegant, ivory-colored invitation addressed to Mister Edgar Van Helsing. "Eddie, what's this?" I waved my discovery in front of him

"Oh, that," he said nonchalantly.

I looked at the name. "Bianca Renfield?" I interrupted him, "the Bianca Renfield of Renfield clothing line?"

"Yeah, she's my grandmere."

"No way! You're related to someone famous? I can't wait to meet her. Is she nice?"

Eddie smiled at my excitement. "Yes, Shell, Grandmere is very nice. It's her invitation to our annual family reunion in two weeks."

I glanced down at the invite. The R.S.V.P. date was today. "Have you called to confirm you're going?"

"Ah, no," he replied. "I was going to ask if you wanted to come with me."

I dropped the card in shock. Meeting the extended family was a huge step. I have only met the Von Stokers, Eddie's aunt and uncle. They are a very nice vampire couple who took Eddie in when he moved to Zephyr about eight years ago. "Sure! I'd love to meet your family."

Eddie's face brightened up. He unclipped his cell phone from the belt of his jeans. "It's going to be a week-long reunion, babe."

"A week-long!" I gasped. "Just what do you do?" Normal family reunions are only one day. But I guess if you're as rich as Bianca Renfield, nothing is normal.

"Catch up with family gossip, eat like kings, go to galas. All rather boring, truth be told."

I rolled my eyes at him. Being related to the woman who owned a multi-million dollar clothing company is boring? I don't think so. "I'll talk with Raquel about it tomorrow at work." I looked at Eddie. "And you need to call your grandmere to confirm our R.S.V.P."

He stepped into another room to make the call as I helped Amelia finish setting the table. We set two bottles of root beer and cola on the table along with ten place settings. Eddie had just finished his phone call when Dad stepped through the doorway with two grocery bags in his hands. "Do you need some help, Mr. Anderson?" Eddie asked.

"No, thanks. I think I've got it, Eddie," Dad said with a smile. "You're going to be my son-in-law soon. You don't need to call me 'Mr. Anderson.' 'Timothy' will do just fine."

"It's just a formality," Eddie said.

"I keep telling him that, Dad," I said as I came into the kitchen, "but he doesn't listen to me."

Dad and Eddie looked at each other. "I see you've already acquired the fine art of not listening," Dad said.

Eddie chuckled. "Unfortunately, it doesn't work too well when you're dating a telepath."

"Very funny, you two." I glanced into the grocery bags. "Geesh, Dad, how many bags do you need for a gallon of milk?"

"I remembered we were out of bread," Dad replied as he began putting away the groceries.

"And eggs, hamburger, and salad fixings, apparently," I observed.

"It's like the chips and salsa emergency we had the other day," Eddie said dryly.

"Running out of chips and salsa is an emergency," I said. I made a detour to the large freezer in search of my birthday cake. "Hey, Dad, what kind of ice cream cake did you get?"

"I don't know. Ask your stepmother. She bought the cake."

"It's vanilla," Amelia said as she came into the kitchen.

I peered at the cake. It was a white sheet cake with purple and green icing with the words Happy Birthday, Shelly written on top. Multicolored flowers lined the edge of the cake. My mouth watered at the sight.

Eddie was peering over my shoulder at the cake. "I say we just skip dinner and go straight for the ice cream cake," he suggested.

"Is that all right with you guys?" I asked.

"And not have this wonderful dinner Amelia and I made for you?" Dad asked teasingly.

Shrugging, I put an arm around my fiancé's waist. "I guess we should consent, Eddie."

The front door opened and in walked my older brother, Robin. Many people have mistaken us for twins with our brown hair and blue eyes, but Robin is a year older. Like my father, he is at least six feet tall. He is a detective with the Zephyr police and likes to be addressed as "Detective Robin Anderson." Eddie and I call it "going into his full-blown cop mode." My brother's magical ability to control and animate plant life does help in his career, especially when he's pursuing criminals. No one likes getting clotheslined by a tree branch. He was wearing a red hooded sweatshirt with a pair of faded jeans and carried a hastily wrapped gift.

Trailing behind him was one of our childhood friends, Roger Miller, talking on his cell phone, to his supermodel elfin girlfriend, Veronica Elfinson. He had a blue envelope in his free hand. "Yeah, Veronica, I like the Armani suit. I'll wear it to court on Monday." Veronica was the three-time winner of the Miss Zephyr Pageant. She is also the producer of the immensely popular TV show, Model Guests, an awful reality show where supermodels live in a mansion (provided by Veronica herself) and compete for the coveted spot as the model of Naughty Angel, Veronica's lingerie line.

Roger works in the district attorney's office, but today, he was wearing designer jeans and an expensive-looking red and green polo shirt. He used to walk with a limp, the result of a gunshot wound, but magical medicine has healed his hip completely. He hung up his phone and said hi to everyone.

"Let me guess, Roger," I said. "You got me a gift certificate."

Roger looked at Robin with his bright green eyes. "You told her, didn't you?"

"No!" Robin protested. "This is Shelly we're talking about."

"How so?" Eddie asked.

Roger and Robin looked at each other. "When we were kids, Shelly would always be snooping around the house to figure out what her presents would be," my brother explained to Eddie.

" 'Snooping' is such a strong word, Robin," I said. "I prefer the term 'covert maneuvers.' "

"Tell me about it. Do you realize how impossible it was to keep the proposal a secret from Shelly, and she can read my mind?" Eddie smiled at me.

"Hey, it's my birthday. I get to guess what presents I get, and nobody can stop me! Bwahaha!"

"Shelly, I think you can wait for another hour and a half," Robin said.

"I don't think so," I replied.

The front door opened, and in stepped Roger's sister, Lisa Miller, and her boyfriend, Dirk Van Helsing, Eddie's older brother. Dirk was dressed in a red polo shirt, jeans, and tan loafers. His shoulder-length, straight black hair was pulled back in its standard ponytail.

Green-eyed Lisa wore a blue blouse, white jeans, and tan pumps. An artificial red rose was clipped in her platinum blonde hair. Lisa made Dirk carry my birthday present, a large, flat box wrapped in pink wrapping paper.

"See, Roger, you should be more like your sister," I said, pointing to the present.

"Why? So, you can get more presents to open?" Roger asked.

"Hey, Roger," Dad called from the kitchen. "When is your father coming over? Never mind."

We all looked out the window and saw the tall, frosted redheaded Bruce get off his green dragon. Bruce was my dad's partner on the police force in my hometown. He sports a hideous, red Tom Selleck mustache and has perpetually angry green eyes. He wore a navy blue, long-sleeved polo shirt, blue jeans, and leather cowboy boots.

The forty-five-year-old former police detective helped his girlfriend, a gorgeous elf, off the dragon. The lithe Libby Elfstar is a nutritionist and an assistant cook at my dad's diner. Instead of her usual white cook's uniform, she wore a knee-length jean skirt, a green cashmere sweater, and ankle boots with a three-inch heel. She had recently cut her blonde hair into a Jackie O-style which complimented her lavender eyes.

Everyone greeted each other once Bruce and Libby got inside. Dad called everyone to the table and we all dug into the scrumptious meal of veggie and pasta primavera, steak, and garlic butter asparagus. Eddie was pouring me a glass of root beer when Dad asked us if we had chosen a wedding date yet. My vampire nearly spilled the soda onto my lap. "Date?" he asked my father.

"Dad," I said catching the bottle, "it's the same thing we told you yesterday. We haven't set one yet."

"I know, but you don't want to wait too long," Dad reminded.

How long did he date your stepmother before they got married? Eddie asked me subliminally.

My answer was kicking him in the shin under the table. "Dad, Eddie and I are going to set a date when we go to his family reunion in a couple of weeks," I replied.

Dad's fork was in mid-air when he looked at the vampire. "And when were you going to tell me this, Eddie?" he asked.

"Uh, sometime this week. I just got the invitation," Eddie lied.

Yeah, last month, I added silently. I could've said more, but Dirk jumped right in.

"I sent my R.S.V.P. three weeks ago," Dirk piped up. "Lisa and I can't go because we're going to a Disc Jockey convention that week."

Eddie shot his brother an irritated look for ousting him. "Okay," he answered. "I just forgot about it."

Bruce narrowed his piercing green eyes at my boyfriend. "And how do you think Timothy's going to find someone to cover for you? Did you think about that, Eddie?" he asked.

"Frankly, Mr. Miller, it's none of your business," Eddie replied. "So butt out."

A spark of electricity flickered off Bruce's clenched fist. He had mastered his electrokinesis, but whenever his temper flares up, electricity fills the air around him. Bruce doesn't like Eddie. He believes Eddie is reckless and dangerous. Not because Eddie's a vampire, but according to Bruce, and I quote, "Eddie is constantly putting Shelly in danger without concern for her well-being." Totally untrue. I'm the one putting myself in danger, and Eddie watches my back. Bruce looked at Dad. "Timothy, you can't possibly let him take a sudden vacation."

"I'll work double shifts to make up for it," Eddie told my father.

"Bruce does have a point, Eddie," Dad said. "This is a sudden vacation."

You're always taking Mr. Miller's side, Eddie thought to himself, not realizing I could read his thoughts. He had a point. Dad tends to take Bruce's point of view, especially when Eddie is involved in the conversation.

I could tell Dad was about to take Bruce's side again. "Dad, I would like to meet his family," I said. Then I added the all-important phrase. "This would mean a lot to me."

Dad couldn't say no to his little girl. He smiled at us. "Well, I guess I can let you go for a week, Eddie. So, tell us about your family."

"Well, my grandmother is Bianca Renfield," Eddie started to say, but Libby cut him off.

"The Bianca Renfield?" she asked.

"Bianca Renfield?" Dad and Bruce asked at the same time.

"Timothy," Amelia said, "every woman knows who Bianca Renfield is. She has her own clothing line."

The light of recognition came on over Dad's and Bruce's heads. "Tell us about this family reunion, Eddie," Dad said.

"It's pretty formal. My grandmere is uber-traditional. She has everyone wear their family colors. Uncle Konrad and Aunt Phoebe, for example, wear some kind of green color."

"What are your family colors, Eddie?" Amelia asked.

"Metallic blue, I think," he answered. "The entire thing is

extremely formal. All the men will be wearing capes."

"Even you?" I asked

"Unfortunately, yes." Vampires don't wear capes on a regular basis. So seeing Eddie in one is a rare and really funny thing. He looks like a leftover cast member for a bad Dracula movie.

"Is it going to have the classic high collar, too?" I asked, a little too excitedly.

He rolled his eyes. He hates the idea of wearing a cape. "Yes. And, no, I won't be speaking in any accent."

"Aw, man," I said. "My dreams of hearing you speak in a bad Dracula voice have shattered once again."

"Shell, you'll have to wear an evening gown in the same color for the three galas."

"I don't have an evening gown, Eddie," I said, hoping to get out of the whole gala. I don't do dressy.

"Not to worry, Shelly," Lisa piped up. "Even though I won't be going, I will certainly help you pick one out at the mall tomorrow night."

Great, there goes half of my paycheck down the drain, I

thought to myself. Lisa has a good, but expensive taste in clothing. No doubt she would drive me to the most expensive store in the mall. (And she was going to be my wedding planner.) I glanced down at my plate. Everyone began talking about different things while we finished our meal. Amelia and Libby began clearing off the table, and then they brought in the cake, along with a huge knife.

Dad took a package of candles out of his pocket, reached over, and began placing the candles on the cake. "Amelia, we need a lighter!" he called my stepmom.

"Libby and I are looking for one, Timothy," she answered as we heard the two women shuffling through various kitchen drawers.

"I got it, Mrs. Anderson," Eddie said. He snapped his fingers over one candle and murmured, "Nebulae." A flicker of white flame suddenly was dancing over the candle. He picked up the lit candle and began setting the others aflame.

"Show off," I told him.

He grinned at me. "How else were you going to blow out your candles?"

Amelia and Libby sat back down and Dad reached across the room and flicked off the lights. Then everyone started singing "Happy Birthday" which was nice because everyone was more or less singing on-key.

Eddie slipped his arm around me and whispered, "What are you going to wish for?"

"What do I need wishes for? I've already got you," I whispered back.

He kissed me but had to stop when Robin shouted for me to blow out the candles. I took a deep breath and then let it go, along with a tiny wad of spittle. All the candles flickered out, and the room was in complete darkness. I heard my brother get up and turn on the light. "Shelly, can I have a piece without spit on it?" Robin asked.

I looked up from cutting the cake. "Do not make fun of people who have knives in their hands," I warned him. I cut a frosting-coated corner piece for Eddie. He has a huge sweet tooth. I cut a big piece for myself before distributing slightly smaller pieces to everyone else. Once I bit into the yummy ice cream cake, I was in cake heaven. "Oh, this is good." I turned to

Eddie. "We should have an ice cream cake at the wedding."

He nodded as he took another bite. "Oh, that's a great idea, babe! We would have to bring it out just a few minutes before the actual cake cutting."

Roger looked at us. "Wouldn't the cake melt?" he asked.

"Well, yeah, but it'd still be cool," I replied with Eddie nodding in agreement.

"I think it's time for presents," Dad said. "Whose presents do you want to open first?"

"Eddie's, of course," I replied. Dad handed me the biggest present. The beautiful wrapping paper didn't last very long because I tore it off. I removed the white gift box's cover and gasped at the genuine black leather messenger bag. "Eddie, this is beautiful."

Eddie took a sip of his iced tea. "There's more inside, babe."

I began unzipping the three main compartments and pulled out a brand-new sketch pad, colored pencils, and a pad of lined paper. So you can write down clues to the next mystery we go on, Eddie had written on the pad. "Thank you, honey. This will fit my laptop perfectly."

Then I pulled out the last present with a perplexed look. It was an old book with red leather binding. Written in pure silver were the words: Knowledge is Power. Without Knowledge, There is no Power. I flipped through the pages to find a book on sword fighting. "Uh, thanks, honey?" I said with uncertainty. I like action movies and all, but a book on sword fighting?

It's for your own protection, Eddie told me sublimely.

I looked at him. *By reading a book on sword fighting?*

I'll explain later.

Everyone oohed and awed over the bag as I held it up for all to see. Eddie was grinning widely as he saw how happy I was with his gift, with the exception of the odd book. Then he leaned back in his chair and got the second present for me.

"Oh, Eddie, you didn't," I said the minute I saw the jewelry. It was a gorgeous necklace with purple and brown gems linked together on a thin gold chain. The brass pendant hanging at the bottom had a star over a triangle engraved in the same purple hue. "This is so beautiful."

"What a lovely necklace, Shelly," Libby said.

"Shelly put it on," Lisa said.

I let Eddie put the necklace on me and then showed it off to everyone. "Isn't this cool? Eddie and I saw it at that new antique shop downtown. Amelia, you'd really like the stuff they have there. They have a couple of paintings you and Dad could put in the living room."

"Eddie, since when do you go antiquing?" Robin asked.

There was no way that he was going to have a reputation as an antique shopper. "One shop, Robin," he answered, holding up an index finger. "It was one shop."

Robin rolled his eyes like he didn't believe him. "You'll never catch me in an antique shop."

"Oh, please," I said, "you would go if Brooke asked you."

My brother was about to protest when Roger chimed in. "She's got a point there, Robin. You would do anything for Brooke."

"Anyway," Eddie said getting back to the subject (me) at hand, "the owner told us this interesting story about the necklace. She got it from this news correspondent who lived in Nehebkau for some time. The necklace is supposed to be something royalty would wear."

Bruce perked up with interest. "Nehebkau? Wasn't your grandfather stationed there for a while, Libby?" he asked.

"A couple of years, I think," she answered.

"Why don't you open some more presents, Shelly?" Dad suggested. He handed me a small square-shaped present. "This is from Amelia and me."

Tearing off the generic birthday paper, I squealed in delight as I noticed the box. "Ooh, a digital camera!" I opened the box and lifted out the small, gray and pink camera case. Unzipping the case, I pulled out a black Viewfinder 2.0.

"That's a sweet camera, Shell," Eddie said, admiring the palm-size camera.

"Let's try it out," I suggested. Hitting the On switch, I turned around in my seat and took a quick picture of Eddie.

The flash was on because the vampire held up his hand to block the sudden white light. "Aah!" he shouted. "Don't blind me."

"Sorry," I said. "But at least, the camera works."

The rest of the presents were rather boring. Bruce and

Libby gave me a gift certificate to a bookstore, as did Roger. Lisa and Dirk gave me a pink and yellow striped sweater. Robin's present was a mystery book I hadn't read yet.

Chapter Two:

How To Shop For a Perfect Dress

The next evening Lisa dragged Eddie, Dirk, and me to the twenty-four-hour Moonlight Mall for our outfits for the family reunion. I wasn't exactly thrilled as we entered Dresses Galore, a discount dress, and accessories store. I just wasn't in the clothes-shopping mood. "Shelly," Lisa said as she began to look through the first rack of evening gowns, "why don't you and I pick out a few dresses for you to try on while Dirk and Eddie get the things Eddie needs for the trip?"

The brothers looked at each other and began to make a break for it when I said, "Whoa, Whoa! Wait just a minute!" There was no way Eddie was leaving me alone. "I think Eddie should stay here and help me pick out the dress he likes the best."

Lisa thought about it for a minute. "Ooh, that's a great idea, Shelly!"

You didn't think that you'd get out of this that easily, I told my future husband.

Crap! Eddie thought.

"All right," Dirk said, "I'm out of here." With that said, he sprinted towards the exit

Lisa held up a metallic blue halter dress with a huge v-neck that plunged past my waist. "What do you think?" she asked.

"Uh," I glanced over at Eddie. *Help!*

"If you were going to the stripper's convention, then yes," he replied, barely looking up from the motorcycle magazine he brought with him.

That pretty much vetoed that dress. "No," I said.

About an hour and ten dresses fit for a Hooters Waitress Convention later, Lisa pawed around the rack and pulled out another dress. It was a metallic blue, sleeveless ball gown with an empire waistline with tiny silver, flower-shaped sequins sparkling in the fluorescent lights of the store. I fell head over heels in love with the dress, and it was the perfect price and size, to boot.

I went into the dressing room. Lisa had picked out a few dress shirts for herself. Eddie found himself in a padded chair and patiently read his magazine after he placed my purse on the floor next to him. As I slipped into the dress, I stared at the beautiful designs and the pretty colors as a grand idea came to me. "Lisa," I called out, "do you have a second? I need my dress zipped."

Lisa pulled back the curtain and looked at me, nodding. "You look beautiful in that dress, Shelly. Eddie will love it," she said as she zipped up the back.

"I think so, too," I replied as we showed Eddie.

He didn't notice me at first. I asked him what he thought of the dress."It looks nice, babe," he responded without looking up from his motorcycle repair article.

"Good," I said convincingly, "because I'm going to put it on your credit card."

"What?" he said, putting the magazine down and giving

me his full attention. His eyes focused on me in the dress as he gave a low whistle. "You look absolutely stunning, babe." He motioned for me to turn around so he could get a better look as he nodded appreciatively. "I like it on you." *You are going to be the most beautiful woman at the gala.*

I felt myself blushing at the telepathic message he sent me. I glanced down at the dress again and remembered my great idea. "Eddie, I know what color we're going to have at the wedding."

"Color?" he asked.

"Yeah, for the theme." How many weddings had he been to? "The color could be metallic blue."

"Ooh!" said Lisa. "That's a pretty color, and I can easily find matching bridesmaids' dresses."

I looked at Eddie. "What do you think of that?"

He shrugged. "Fine with me, but I'm not wearing a metallic blue tuxedo. I don't think dressing like a pimp would be appropriate for our wedding."

I shook my head at him and kissed him. "Why would I do that to you, honey? The tie or some other accessory will be metallic blue."

Lisa called Dirk and asked him to meet Eddie in Tally's, a department store at the other end of the mall. Eddie needed to pick up some new dress shirts and a couple of new ties. My fiancé kissed me goodbye and reluctantly went off to join his brother.

"Shelly, we've got to get you some shoes to match that dress," Lisa told me as we walked to the shoe department.

The next two weeks were very busy as I got ready for the trip. I was fairly nervous about meeting the rich and famous family of my future husband. Would they like me? Uncle Konrad and Aunt Phoebe already agreed I was a perfect match for their nephew.

Much to my father's disappointment, Eddie and I still hadn't decided on a date for the wedding. I hadn't seen my fiancé since the shopping trip. He had been working double shifts to make up for his sudden vacation and was sleeping every minute he could.

On the night we were leaving for Carpathia, I finished

packing my bags just as Eddie arrived to pick me up. I grabbed

the strange book the vampire had given me and threw it in my

suitcase. I greeted him in a new pair of Leviathan jeans, a green

sweatshirt, and sneakers. As I quickly kissed him, I inhaled the

scent of Blue Ice, his favorite cologne. "Hello, honey," I told him.

"Hello, babe," he said as he shoved his hands into the

pockets of his black jeans. Underneath his jean jacket, he wore a

brand-new maroon polo shirt. "We ready to go?" he asked.

"Almost," I said as I struggled with the zipper on my

suitcase.

"Allow me, Shelly." With one swift tug and using only a

third of his strength, he managed to close the suitcase. "What

are you packing?"

"Clothes," I answered.

"We're only going to be there for a week, babe."

I grabbed my purple garment bag and the new laptop bag

as Eddie took my black, rolling suitcase. "Yeah, but I didn't have

time to downsize my toiletry bags. They take up a lot of room,

you know."

"One day, I'm going to show you the art of compact

packing," he said jokingly as we headed out the door. I ran through a mental checklist to make sure I hadn't forgotten anything. Dad and Amelia would feed my winged horse, Jordan. I had everything I needed, including my cell phone and charger. I was good to go.

I locked up, and we headed out to where Eddie's orange carrot-shaped car sat idling in my driveway. Because the vampire is a vegetarian, he has built all of his seven cars in the shapes of various fruits and vegetables. His carrot car is his absolute favorite because he has won several races with it. We tossed my bags into the back seat next to Eddie's blue duffle and garment bags and got into the car.

"So, are we still meeting the Count and Countess at the train station?" I asked as he backed the car out of my driveway.

Eddie nodded. "Actually, we're running a bit late. I overslept," he explained as he hit the accelerator. Even when he isn't on the racing track, he still has a lead foot.

I instinctively buckled my seatbelt. Normally it takes half an hour to get to the train station, but we arrived there in ten minutes flat. I glanced behind to see if any police patrols were following us. "One of these days, you're going to get pulled over."

"Haven't yet," Eddie said with a confident tone. "Plus, if I do, I can get out of it by blackmailing Robin."

"Ooh," I said, perking up at the chance of blackmailing my own flesh and blood. "I've plenty of dirt on Robin." We got out of the car and Eddie and I grabbed our bags. The blue marble building was loud as trains screeched by, picking up and dropping off their passengers at the two platforms. When we entered the revolving glass doors, I looked up at the sky-high LCD screens depicting the departure and arrival times. The train to Carpathia was leaving in about thirty minutes. That gave us barely enough time to pick up the tickets, check our bags, and walk across the huge station before the last boarding call.

"Two round-trip tickets for Carpathia, please," Eddie told the elf clerk at the ticket counter as he fished his wallet from his back pocket. "They're under the name Eddie Van Helsing." He pulled out his identification card with his picture. All residents of Zephyr are required to have some kind of picture ID card.

The lady began typing on her computer and within a few minutes had found our reservations. "Eddie Van Helsing and

Shelly Anderson?”

"Yes," Eddie and I replied at the same time as I showed her my ID card and told her we were checking two bags each.

The lady printed out our tickets and four temporary sticker baggage tags with our destination. She slid the tags through the handles of the baggage just before she gave us our tickets. "Have a nice trip."

As Eddie and I said our thanks, his cell phone rang. He unclipped it from his belt and answered it. "Uncle Konrad, we're at the ticket counter. You and Aunt Phoebe are already on board. Which car are you guys in? The dining car. Shelly and I will be there in a few minutes." He put away his phone. "We've got to get going, Shell," he told me.

I handed my suitcase and garment bag to a centaur who had already grabbed Eddie's bags. Then we began to book it down the long platform as a booming voice told us over the loudspeaker our train was making its final boarding call. My fiancé sprinted down the aisle with the speed of a marathon runner. I, on the other hand, was slowed down by the weight of my laptop bag and my purse. "Eddie!" I shouted. "Slow down!"

He skidded to a stop, realized I wasn't right behind him, and ran back. "Give me your laptop, Shelly," he said. I graciously handed him the bag, and he hoisted it over his shoulder. Then he grabbed my hand, and we ran to catch our train.

The big, black locomotive was starting to roll down the platform when Eddie jumped over the small set of stairs in one gracious leap, landing on the train perfectly. I was still on the platform, only a few steps behind him. With one swift motion, he pulled me up beside him.

A strand of my brown hair had fallen into my face, and I tucked it behind my ear. "That was cool!" I said, impressed.

"What? Me pulling you onto the train?" he asked as we walked into the dining car.

"Yeah, it was almost like a romantic scene from an action movie. But what would have made it better was if the train was moving much faster."

He raised an eyebrow at me. "Seeing you get sucked under the train would have been romantic."

"Hey, let me have my own unrealistic, romantic moments. Thank you very much."

Before we entered the dining car, a stocky werebear in a charcoal gray conductor's uniform was blocking the inner door to the car. He had seen us leap onto the train and gruffly demanded our tickets. After we handed him our tickets, he gave us back the stubs and stepped aside.

I gasped in awe when I noticed the layout of the dining car. *Wow, this is impressive*, I told Eddie telepathically. The wall of the dining car was painted a glossy black. The ten windows on each side of the car sat above each one of the twenty booths. The rich, red leather seats of the booths themselves were much nicer than the ones at Dad's diner. The wrought iron tables were completely devoid of tablecloths or vases of flowers.

About half of the booths were filled with members of the undead. A group of four werewolves in their business suits and full wolf form were discussing the lectures they would be attending at their convention. Sitting about three booths away was a group of three vampire frat boys who were privately discussing their plans for spring break. I scrunched up my face as I discovered what those plans entailed. *They are **so** underage,* I said half to myself and half to Eddie.

Eddie glanced at me. *Problems, Shelly?* he asked telepathically.

I just found out what those kids are doing on spring break.

Let me guess. Sex, drugs, and alcohol.

I nodded. *But even more.*

He made a face. *Eew!*

"Shelly! Eddie!" someone called us.

We both looked up and saw a balding, overweight vampire wearing a plaid flannel shirt and a pair of suspenders holding up his black slacks and waving to us. Eddie walked up to him and immediately received a big bear hug from his uncle, Count Konrad Van Stoker. "So glad you made it on time, Eddie," he said.

A vampire wearing a bright blue dress and white shawl got up from her seat next to the Count. The Countess Phoebe Von Stoker is a dead ringer for Morticia Addams but always wears very vibrant colors. "Shelly, Eddie, dears!" she said to us.

I hugged her. Looking at Eddie, I jerked my head for him to follow suit. "How are you doing, Countess?" I asked her.

"Very good, Shelly, and please call me 'Aunt Phoebe.

You're going to be a part of our family and don't need to call me 'Countess.'"

"And don't call me 'Count' either. 'Uncle Konrad' is what I want you to call me from now on." He turned to his wife. "I don't know why we even have these titles. They're quite silly."

Aunt Phoebe shook her head. "It's tradition, my dear."

"I will, Aunt Phoebe and Uncle Konrad," I said. "You should take a lesson from her, Eddie."

Eddie hugged his aunt. "Very funny, Shelly."

Aunt Phoebe looked at us with her soft brown eyes. "Is this a private joke between you two?" she asked us.

I smiled. "No, my dad's been trying to get Eddie to call him by his first name, instead of calling him Mr. Anderson."

"Well, it's a little hard because he's also my boss."

Aunt Phoebe smiled at us. "I'm so sorry, but Konrad and I must leave you two. The engineer, an old friend of ours, has invited us to eat with him in his private dining car."

"That's all right, Aunt Phoebe," Eddie assured her. "Shelly and I will be just fine."

Uncle Konrad looked at me before they left. "I would try

the scrambled vulture eggs," he told me.

Eddie frantically shook his head at me. *Don't. They're so disgusting. Very, very runny.*

"I'll keep that in mind, Uncle Konrad," I said as I sat down.

Once they were gone, Eddie took off the messenger bag and handed it to me. Then he slid into the seat across from me. "Trust me, the eggs are nasty."

I looked at the menu. Most of the stuff is advertised as fine dining for the undead. "Okay, what do you recommend?"

"Their pizza's pretty decent, and you have to try a cup of Transylvanian mint chocolate coffee."

"Ooh, mint chocolate coffee! I have to have that!"

Our waiter was a young vampire in her late teens. With her long black hair, pale makeup, black lipstick, and multiple piercings, she definitely screamed "goth." Pulling out her pad and pen, she gave us the apathetic look of every overworked, unappreciated, underpaid food service employee before asking what we wanted. "What do you want?"

"We'll have two cups of Transylvanian mint chocolate coffee and a medium cheese pizza," Eddie said to her.

"No blood?" she asked.

"No, thank you."

She trudged off with our orders. Once she was out of earshot, I leaned over the table and whispered to Eddie, "She sounds so happy in her job."

"Yeah, I could see the joy bursting from her eyes, and her enthusiasm. That was something else."

I was about to add something when our cell phones began buzzing. I fished mine out of my purse and saw I had a text message from my brother. "Robin texted me."

Eddie had unclipped his cell phone from his belt and was reading his message as well. "Me too."

We compared messages that said the exact same thing: When are you guys going to set a date? I rolled my eyes. "This is the fifth time this week someone asked me when our wedding is going to be."

"Me too. It's mainly your dad and your stepmom who've been doing the asking. 'So, when's the big day?' 'Have you talked to Shelly about the wedding?' 'You guys shouldn't wait too long.'"

I smiled. "That sounds like Dad, but we do need to set a date."

"We've got a four-hour train ride. That should give us plenty of time."

I got out my day calendar and opened it up. "I've been thinking about it," I started to say.

"I'm sure you have," Eddie replied.

"Well, I don't want the wedding to be during winter. It's too cold."

Eddie nodded in agreement. "You'd complain about the cold. What about spring?"

"Nah, I think that's kind of trendy."

"Okay, but summer's out as well. Dirk mentioned to me Lisa is all booked up for the summer months. How about a fall wedding? A lot of people could make it, and it won't be too cold or too hot."

I thought about it for a few minutes. A fall wedding would be lovely and unique in my family. My dad's first wedding was in the early summer, and his second wedding took place right before Christmas. "That's a great idea, hon. Most of the places and people, like the catering and the chapel, will have openings.”

“What about the reception?”

“I asked Dad if we could use the diner for the reception.”

“Good idea, babe. It’ll save us some money.”

I nodded. “Exactly.”

He leaned over. “Hey, I want to plan our honeymoon.”

I smiled at him. “So, where are you thinking?”

He grinned. “I have a few places in mind. Let me think about it for a while.”

Our waitress came back. She slammed down a pot of delicious-smelling coffee and creamer on the table and then shoved the cups on the table before trudging off again. “Thank you,” I said, but she never heard me.

Eddie poured coffee for both of us. Then he added cream and three packets of sugar in each cup. He watched me take a sip of the coffee. “What do you think?” he asked.

“This is the best coffee I’ve ever had,” I said as I took another sip, being careful not to scorch the roof of my mouth. “I need to find a way to have it shipped to Zephyr.”

“Perhaps Grandmere can help with that,” Eddie replied.

I nodded in agreement. "Okay, let's get back to the subject at hand. We need to set a date. How does September sound?"

"Not October?"

"Too late in the fall. Plus, don't you think if we had it around Halloween, it would be kind of cheesy?"

He thought about it for a moment. "Good point."

We looked at the calendar opened to September. It took us a minute or so, but we finally decided on the 18th of September, the first Saturday in the one month when the leaves change colors. I took out my laptop and proceeded to open it up. Last week, I set up a spreadsheet so we could put together a budget for the wedding. I had written down a list of things that we needed to purchase. Moving over to Eddie's seat, I showed him what I did.

"Wow!" he said after looking at the document. "Excellent work, babe."

"Thank you. It took me about three hours to put this thing together." I typed in a note indicating we would use the diner for the reception. "So, I'm excited about meeting the rest of your family."

"Don't be."

"Why?"

"I'm going to warn you about my family."

I raised an eyebrow. "That doesn't sound good."

"My family is-." He paused as he tried to find the right word. Finally, he settled on one. "Unique."

"Ooh," I said rubbing my hands together, "I hear a story coming."

After our waiter came by with our food, Eddie gave a great sigh. "Here are the rules concerning my family. Remember to compliment my Aunt Antonia on what she is wearing, even if it is hideous. Do not, under any circumstances, ask Uncle Philip about his business. Because if you do, he will not shut up about it. Beware of my Uncle Dracul. He drank some infected human blood about a hundred years ago and has been a little crazy ever since."

"Please, Eddie, I can handle crazy. I work at the library remember."

"Yes, but has anyone ever tried to bite you without warning?"

"Good God, no! Does he really do that?"

"He has tried several times. He's an old vampire, almost nine hundred years old, and is getting to be senile. So, be careful around him."

"Oh, come on, Eddie! They can't be that bad." I said. "You're making your family out to be dysfunctional."

"You don't know the half of it," he muttered under his breath.

I pushed his snarky remark out of my mind. Every person overreacts when describing their family. For the rest of the trip, we talked about our upcoming wedding until I drifted off to sleep against Eddie's shoulder, lulled by the gentle rocking of the train.

Chapter Three:
Eddie's Grandparents and Their McMansion

"Shelly, we're here!" Eddie said, gently nudging me awake.

I opened my eyes and found the outside of the train completely dark. "What time is it?" I asked.

Eddie checked his watch. "Seven o'clock."

"But why is it so dark?"

"We're in Carpathia, remember? It is dark all the time here."

I noticed that my computer was gone. I glanced up at the smiling Eddie. He had put it away after I fell asleep. "Shall we?" I asked him.

"Let's."

We picked up our luggage and joined Uncle Konrad and

Aunt Phoebe outside the stately, old Carpathia train station.

A black and gold carriage pulled by a pair of black unicorns came to a halt a few inches in front of us. A ghost dressed in a blood-red colonial footman's uniform was driving the carriage. "Count and Countess Van Stoker and guests, I presume?" he asked us.

"Yes, Henry," Uncle Konrad replied as he and Eddie put away our bags on the back of the carriage. Inside the carriage were two plush black velvet seats facing each other. Aunt Phoebe and Uncle Konrad sat on one seat and Eddie joined me on the other bench.

Henry snapped the reins, and the unicorns began trotting down the street. Pulling back the curtain, I got a good look at the town as we headed toward Bianca Renfield and Rudolf Harker's home. One look around the small town told me they were a powerful influence here. Stately colonials and large department stores dotted the streets of Carpathia. The carriage took a sharp turn and began moving up a long hill. I gasped as I stared at the house.

Eddie joined me at the window. "Everything all right?" he

asked softly.

"Yeah," I replied, still staring at the huge four-story Italian gothic mansion looming impressively over the entire town. "I thought your house was huge."

"Fifty bedrooms with their bathrooms."

"Sweet deal!"

"Maybe we should buy a house like that."

"Good God, no! I can barely keep my apartment clean." I stared out the window at the towering factory building that was coming up on our right. Bright neon lights signified it was the Renfield, Inc., main building.

It's a good thing that Grandmere always gives a tour of her factory and store, Eddie told me.

That brought a smile to my face. I leaned against my fiancé's shoulder. I was going to be marrying into wealth. Well, not directly.

The carriage crossed a rickety-covered bridge over an overflowing river. According to Aunt Phoebe, the river, Tepes, overflows every year with torrential rainfall. We finally came to a halt. I peered out the window and watched the eight-foot-high iron gates open up for us. Henry snapped the reins, and the

carriage began the long ascent up the paved driveway. It finally

stopped in front of the huge house with six pillars that would

have made the ancient Greeks envious. The four-story building

was made entirely of golden bricks and black siding. It looked

like each bedroom had its own balcony. Man, for the next week, I

was going to be living like a queen. Eddie nudged me out of my

fantasy and handed me my garment bag.

Pulling off the strongman routine very nicely, the vampire

grabbed my last bag and his two bags and flung them easily over

his shoulder. Uncle Konrad and Aunt Phoebe shared only one

bag and Uncle Konrad easily grabbed the huge leather suitcase.

We walked up the large, black marble stairs to the two,

twelve-foot, munco tree doors. Uncle Konrad gave the ring on

the brass lion's head door knocker three firm knocks. I expected

the sounds to echo throughout the house, but they seemed

muffled by the sudden, loud footsteps heading toward the door.

We all stepped back as the doors swung open, revealing

a very tall, pale green man dressed in a charcoal gray tuxedo. A

white hand towel was draped over the left arm of this dead ringer for Frankenstein's monster, complete with neck bolts and a scar on his forehead. "Good evening, Count and Countess," he said with a slight bow of respect to the older vampires.

"Good evening, Jeffers," Uncle Konrad said.

The butler looked down at Eddie and me. "It's good to see you again, Mister Edgar."

"Good to see you, too, Jeffers," Eddie replied as he shook the big man's hand after setting the bags down. Then he placed his free hand around my waist. "This is my fiancée, Shelly."

When the sleeve of his suit coat rode up, I noticed the butler's hand was stitched on. I had never seen a Frankenstein monster before, so, I was a bit shocked. Eddie had to nudge me again so I could shake Jeffers' hand. "Hello," I said, quietly.

"Which bedrooms are we going to be staying in?" Uncle Konrad asked Jeffers.

"The same rooms as before," Jeffers replied as he took our bags from us. "Follow me."

He led the four of us up a winding black marble stair with a burgundy carpet running up the middle. When we got to the top, the floor split into two hallways. Each hall was lined with midnight blue and black striped wallpaper and dark cherry

wooden floors. Twelve bedrooms lined each hall. I was able to

peer over the dark cherry wooden railing down towards the front

door.

Jeffers led us to the last bedroom on the left. "This is

where you will be staying, miss," he told me as he opened up the

door. The room with an adjacent balcony was beautifully

decorated. Hanging from a chain in the ceiling, a glistening

cobweb canopy was suspended by a heavy rod iron ring hung

over a huge, four-poster bed almost filling the entire room. An

elegant red and black tulip quilt lay across the bed just waiting

for me to crawl under the covers. The dark, tall cherry wardrobe

was nestled in one of the corners. A full-length mirror with black,

wrought iron edging stood in another corner next to the black

pleather couch.

I even had my bathroom with one of those old-fashioned

claw-foot tubs. It was nice until I saw the dolls. The five-shelf

cherry bookcase was filled with dolls of all shapes and sizes. I

have slight pediophobia, most likely caused by the possessed

doll I had dealt with over Christmas.

I turned around and walked back out to the hall where Eddie was waiting for me. "I can't sleep in there," I whispered to my fiancé.

"Why is that?" Eddie asked.

"Dolls."

He looked at the butler who was patiently waiting for us. "Jeffers, Shelly has a slight doll phobia. Is there any other room she could stay?"

"There is your room," Jeffers suggested.

Eddie shook his head. "That's not going to be an option." He shot me a grin. "Yet."

Jeffers hesitated. "Well, Lukon and his guest were going to stay here, but they changed rooms."

"Okay," Eddie answered, not happy with that answer. He and his cousin had a history and not a very good one.

Jeffers beckoned us up another flight of stairs with the same layout as the second floor. He showed Uncle Konrad and Aunt Phoebe to their room. It could've been a presidential suite in a five-star hotel with its blood-red and black color scheme and the king-sized canopy bed.

Then we walked to Eddie's room. Eddie was about to knock when we heard giggling coming from behind the door. He looked at Jeffers. "If that's who I think it is, then I want a room change."

The butler knocked firmly on the door. "Mister Lukon? Is that you?"

The door swung open and Eddie's cousin stuck his head out the door. He was wearing a short, silk bathrobe and had a very scantily clad lady vampire hanging off him. "Yes, Jeffers?" he asked with an innocent smile." The blond vampire turned to his cousin. "Hey, Eddie, your bed is great."

Eddie cringed. "Is there another room?" he asked Jeffers. *Please let there be another room*, I could mentally hear him praying.

The butler nodded, his face showing no trace of emotion. "We do have the trophy room available." He led us back down to the second floor. Two doors down from the freaky doll room, Jeffers showed us another bedroom. Covering the oak sleigh bed was a king-size plaid comforter set with forest green, red, and navy blue colors. A matching, five-drawer dresser, a full-length mirror, and a navy blue microfiber couch filled up the rest of the room. Like my room, there was a bathroom and a private balcony.

"So, this is the trophy room," I said as I looked around at all the animal heads mounted on the walls. There were all sorts of dragons, manticores, and griffins. The most impressive one was the huge, mean-looking emerald green dragon head staring down at whoever slept in the bed.

"We could switch rooms," Eddie suggested to me.

I hesitated. I've always found taxidermy on the same unsettling scale as wax museum figures and ventriloquist dummies. I wasn't looking forward to waking up in the middle of the night to find myself staring up at a creepy, dead dragon head.

Fortunately, Jeffers came up with a satisfying solution. "I could have all the dolls put up in the attic, Miss Shelly."

"That'd be great," I said with a sigh of relief.

Eddie set his bags on the bed. "Everything looks good, Jeffers."

"Very well, Master Edgar. I will—What the dickens?" he asked as the sound of a gong rang throughout the building. "Who would be using the delivery bell this late in the evening?" he walked down the stairs towards the front door.

"If I didn't know you, Eddie," I said as I reached up and ran my fingers through his black, curly hair, "I'd say that you were reading Jeffers' mind."

He chuckled softly as his finger traced my jawline. "I wish, but, no. Jeffers always asks if the room suits my needs." He kissed me softly on the lips and was about to kiss me again when we heard loud arguing coming from downstairs. We broke away from each other and headed out to the hall.

Peering over the railing, we saw Jeffers and a tall, elegantly dressed vampire with very pale, almost white skin arguing with each other over a long, coffin-shaped box. The rich vampire grabbed his black cape with its crimson redlining and wrapped it around his arm. "Jeffers, you fool, I told you not to sign for any packages for me. This is a very special package, and I have to be the one to sign for it!"

"Sir, I was only doing my job," Jeffers replied without emotion. But his shoulders tensed slightly at the harshness of the vampire's voice.

"If I had it my way, I would have fired you on the spot for your incompetence!"

"Then you should take it up with Mrs. Renfield and Mr. Harker." With that, Jeffers turned smartly on his heel and began walking away.

"Not so fast, Jeffers!" snapped the vampire. "You and Fritz have to take this up to my room now!"

I looked at Eddie who had joined me at the banister. "Who is that guy?" I asked.

"The Baron Ludwig von Bela, the world's greatest opera singer, a family friend to Grandmere and Grandfather, and an all-around jerk."

"I like him already," I said sarcastically.

We peered over the banister and saw a werewolf come out of nowhere to help Jeffers lift the box. If Danny of the T-Birds was a werewolf, he would have looked exactly like this guy, complete with the outfit and everything. He even walked with that little saunter Danny was known for as they carried the box up the stairs.

"Fritz, be careful!" snapped Ludwig.

Eddie and I stepped back to make room for them as they made their way up the second set of stairs.

"Edgar, out of my way," Ludwig snapped at Eddie as he looked right past me and marched off to his room. It was as if I didn't exist.

"Yeah, it's nice to see you, too, Uncle Ludwig," Eddie muttered under his breath. He checked his watch. "I suppose we should get ready for the ball."

I gave him a quick kiss. "I'll meet you out here in about thirty minutes," I told him. I opened the door to my bedroom and walked over to my bed where Eddie had put the bags. I opened the garment bag and pulled out my new dress, the metallic blue color shimmering under the bedroom lights. Then I opened my suitcase and got out my cosmetics bag, nylons, and new silver flats. After redoing my hair and my makeup, I put my nylons on without one snag. My dress was a bit tricky, but I managed to zip it up all the way. Then I looked in the mirror. This outfit was going to knock Eddie off his feet!

When I walked out of my room, Eddie was sitting on a cushioned bench waiting for me. As he stood, a long black cape with a metallic blue lining fell to his ankles. The high neckline reached just past the tops of his ears. He wore a black suit with a white shirt and a black vest. In place of a tie, a metallic blue sash came across his chest complemented by a matching cummerbund.

"Wow!" I said. "Now I know why vampires never wear capes. It just sent you centuries back in time. It's not that bad. I think you look rather dashing."

"I look ridiculous in this getup," he informed me. He scratched the back of his neck. "And this cape itches, too."

"You look incredibly handsome. I love the vest on you. I think you should wear one with your tux for the wedding."

"Thank you, my dear," he said with a smile as he looked me up and down, nodding his head in approval. "You, on the other hand, look positively beautiful tonight." He took my arm. "Come, my love, our coach awaits."

Uncle Konrad and Aunt Phoebe had already taken a coach to the Civic Center, giving Eddie and me a chance to ride by ourselves in a two-person coach driven by a werewolf named

Pierre. He spoke only a few words of English, but his native language was very similar to French. This allowed us to talk about my telepathy.

"Eddie," I said softly, "I'm a little nervous."

"About what? Meeting my family?"

"That and my telepathy. I don't know how I'm going to be able to control it. I'm going to be in a room full of the undead. I'm going to lose my mind."

Eddie put an arm around my shoulder. He hadn't realized how much it would bother my mind reading. "It must drive you crazy to walk into a room full of the undead."

"It's like looking into everyone's private diaries."

"I bet it's not pretty."

"I can handle a few minds, but I get nervous when the room is full of them."

"Does ignoring it help?"

"Somewhat."

"Remember what I told you when you first found out you could read minds."

"Yeah, you told me to focus on a few minds at a time, and

if it gets too much, ignore the minds.”

We rode in silence for a few moments. I was content with Eddie’s advice and hoped it would work. Within a few minutes, we arrived at the ball. Eddie got out first and then took my hand to help me out. The Carpathia Event Center was a beautiful brick, one-story building. The lobby was decorated with hunter-green walls and dark grey carpeting. We got in line behind a large group of finely dressed vampires, werepeople, and one Frankenstein monster.

A ghost, dressed in a long-tailed tuxedo and a top hat, was announcing the guests entering a nearby room. Waltz music wafted from the room. The first announcement we heard was for a vampire couple. The stout man was wearing a grey suit that sharply contrasted with his reddish-brown hair. His black cape, lined with a traditional Scottish color pattern, was wrapped around his left arm. He led his wife, a tall vampire, with his other hand. She wore a long, green evening gown with black, silk chiffon sleeves. “The Laird and Lairdess Duncan MacBlood!” the ghost announced.

My Uncle Duncan and Aunt Penelope, Eddie told me.

The next couple were vampires, as well. The man was wearing a black suit and chocolate brown cape and had a chocolate brown Stetson on his head. His black leather cowboy boots clicked on the marble floor of the civic center lobby.

His wife was wearing a long dark brown satin dress with a halter top. Her black hair was pulled into a tight bun with not one piece of hair out of its place. She looked like a no-nonsense woman with her pure white, expensive-looking pearls.

The ghost made another announcement. "The Duke and Duchess Philip Seward!"

My Uncle Philip and Aunt Antonia, Eddie explained.

The one who will not shut up about his business and the one who must be complimented on what she is wearing?

Eddie nodded.

Who's the tall, green man right behind them? I pointed to the Frankenstein monster in a navy blue pinstripe suit. By his side was a hunchbacked man in a faded yellow tweed suit.

That's Dr. Herman von Karloff, Grandmere and Grandfather's family doctor, and his assistant, Mr. Snerdly.

Since when do vampires need a doctor? They can heal on

their own. I kept that thought to myself. I barely heard the other names being announced as Eddie tried to explain who was who, but I eventually lost track. Finally, we arrived at the door.

"Name?" the ghost asked.

"Edgar Van Helsing and Michelle Anderson," Eddie said.

"Mister Edgar Van Helsing and Miss Michelle Anderson!"

"Next year it'll be Mr. and Mrs. Edgar Van Helsing," Eddie whispered to me with a wink.

"I can't wait," I replied with a smile. With our arms linked, we walked into the huge ballroom. Off to the right was a small orchestra consisting of living skeletons playing a lively waltz. The color scheme of the room matched the lobby. Hunter green curtains were hanging gallantly across the windows. Vampires and Werepeople filled the dance floor. Suddenly, everyone was looking at us, me in particular. That's when I realized I was the only living person in the entire ballroom, and all the blood-drinking vampires were wishing neck-biting was back in style. Creepy.

Eddie noticed me gripping his hand a little too hard. *What's wrong, Shelly?*

Your relatives are staring at me like I'm their next midnight snack. It's a little creepy.

Don't worry. They'll soon know you're my arm candy.

Don't ever refer to me as your arm candy!

Eddie grinned. *Sorry, it slipped out.* The music started again. He bowed to me. "May I have this dance, Miss Anderson?"

"Certainly, Mr. Van Helsing."

Neither one of us are very good dancers, but we managed not to stumble over each other. I felt Eddie's hand on the small of my back as he took my hand. "Have you been practicing, hon?" I asked as his feet glided effortlessly across the floor.

"A little here and there." He looked around the room and then back at me. "I must say, you are the most beautiful woman here tonight."

"That's very sweet of you, Eddie, but are you trying to make up for that 'arm candy' remark?"

Eddie gave a sheepish grin. "True on both accounts." We danced around the ballroom, with everyone looking at us. I felt proud to be dancing with my future husband, not caring I wasn't even undead.

The musicians suddenly stopped in mid-waltz as a loud commotion came from the lobby. Uncle Ludwig was arguing with a pixie. "Where is she, Newton?" he demanded.

"I don't know, sir," the six-inch-tall man said, his dragonfly wings making the only noise in the empty room. "She said she would be here."

"It's just like Justine to make me look bad in front of anyone," he shouted. Then he realized everyone was staring at him. "What's wrong with everyone? Do you like to eavesdrop on conversations that are none of your business?" he snapped.

The music started again. Everything was as before. "Who's Justine?" I asked Eddie.

"I think she's Uncle Ludwig's wife."

"Their marriage is on the rocks."

"You got that from reading Ludwig's mind?"

I nodded. "That and the way he talked about her. What about the pixie?"

"Ludwig's personal assistant, I think." Just then he spotted a small table on the left side of the ballroom. "Shall we waltz over to the hors d'oeuvres?" he suggested.

"Oh, yes," I said with relief. "I'm starving." We discreetly slipped to the back of the room where we dined on little crackers topped with smoked salmon, caviar, deviled quail eggs, jumbo shrimp with cocktail sauce, spinach puffs, cubes of imported cheeses, and slices of various kinds of meat impaled with toothpicks, sushi rolls, egg rolls, fresh veggies with roasted garlic hummus, and prosciutto with melon.

"Edgar!" an elegantly dressed vampire in her mid-six-hundreds (that's mid-sixties in human years!) called to us. She seemed to glide in her pale blue Victorian dress. Her silver hair was pulled up in a bun. "It's so good to see you."

"Grandmere!" Eddie put down the glass of punch and hugged Bianca Renfield. "Thank you for inviting us. Wonderful gala, as usual."

"Why thank you," she said. Then she looked at me with her grey eyes. "And who is this lovely lady I saw you dancing with?"

"Grandmere, this is my fiancée, Shelly Anderson," Eddie replied as he put an arm around me.

"It's a pleasure to meet you, Miss Anderson. I'm so glad Edgar has finally decided to settle down." She smiled warmly at me as she shook my hand. *Edgar has picked out a sweet and pretty bride. She makes him so happy,* she thought with a smile.

"Thank you," I stammered. I was awestruck by meeting the world-famous fashion designer, and a simple thank-you was all I could muster.

A smile crossed the vampire's face. "Miss Anderson, have you picked out a wedding dress yet?"

"Not yet."

"Well, one of my stores is having its grand opening. I would like you and Edgar to join Rudolf and me and see my new line of wedding dresses."

My mouth dropped in surprise. I had never been to a Renfield's store grand opening before and never would have had the opportunity to look at Renfield wedding dresses. "I-I mean we-would love to." I looked at Eddie who nodded yes.

"Good, we will discuss it more after dinner tonight," Bianca said goodbye to us as another business associate called to her.

I turned to Eddie. "That was so nice of your grandmother

to let us look at her line of wedding dresses.”

Eddie resumed drinking his punch. “I told you she was nice.”

“She’s happy for us, and she thinks I make you happy.”

He gave me a peck on the cheek. “You do make me very happy,” he whispered in my ear. “Shall we go for another dance?”

Chapter Four:
An Awkward Family Affair

Before I met the rest of Eddie's family, I had envisioned a group of vampires as kind and caring as my future husband. Boy, was I ever wrong!

Dinner at the Renfield and Harker mansion was at eight o'clock sharp. Eddie and I were still wearing our clothes from the gala, but Eddie opted to take off his cape. We walked downstairs to the dining room.

The room was gorgeous. White cobweb tinsel and giant black caterpillar silk glimmered with faux glass beads resembling early evening dewdrops. Two dazzling crystal chandeliers with tiny light bulbs illuminated the room. Cherry wooden chairs were all around the long table covered with black silk tablecloths with wine-colored flowers in crystal vases. Flickering taper candles gave off a faint apple cinnamon scent. Eddie pulled out my chair and then sat down next to me.

I looked around the table at the other guests and realized Eddie and I were not the only young people present. Lukon was there with the same woman we had seen earlier. I tried to place her. Where had I seen her before? Then it dawned on me. *Eddie, do you recognize that lady with Lukon?*

Yeah, she seems kind of familiar.

Your old couch.

Eddie gasped in shock. *That's Bunny, the hooker he slept with.*

I nodded, grimacing. Then I continued to look around the table. Uncle Philip and Aunt Antonia sat directly across from us. On their left was an annoyed Uncle Ludwig with Newton chattering by his shoulder. Uncle Konrad, Aunt Phoebe, Uncle Duncan, and Aunt Penelope were sitting near Bianca and her husband, Rudolf Harker. Rudolf looked every bit like a Southern gentleman with his white beard and mustache and his tailored charcoal suit. I was disappointed to learn Uncle Dracul hadn't come to the reunion.

Jeffers and two vampire servants began to serve the dinner. For the vegetarians at the table, it was roasted eggplant with parmesan cheese. For the meat-eaters, it was roast duck dipped in pineapple sauce with a side of brown rice and a vegetable medley. Bianca spoke first. "Duncan and Penelope, I understand Martina and Riley were not able to make it."

"Yes, Riley had a modeling tour he couldn't miss, and Martina wasn't feeling well," Penelope replied. The part about Martina was a lie. Both Penelope and Duncan didn't want the family to know that their daughter was going through a nasty divorce, and I certainly wasn't going to spread that news around, along with the announcement that I could read the minds of everyone at the table.

"Mother, guess what!" Aunt Antonia said. "Phillip's company has been rated the number one in blood production."

"For the 70th year in a row!" Uncle Phillip added haughtily. He drank a glass of his company's King Phillip's Blood. "You know, most of the other blood production companies aren't as superior as mine. We don't add any natural ingredients to the blood. It's all chemicals making our product the purest in the market.”

“But wouldn’t adding natural ingredients make the blood pure?” I asked. “Correct me if I’m wrong, but dumping chemicals in the product doesn’t make it pure.”

“You are wrong,” Uncle Philip snapped at me.

Bianca and Rudolf both raised an eyebrow. They clearly weren’t buying the fact King Philip’s Blood was any different from other kinds of blood. “She does have a point, Phillip,” Bianca said wearily.

“She is not one of us, and I do not have to answer her,” Phillip retorted.

Someone needs to be shoved off his high horse, I shared with Eddie

Agreed, Eddie said. *You’re the first person who has challenged Uncle Phillip about his blood company.*

Bianca was already tired of listening to Phillip. “Edgar, don’t you have some news for us?”

Eddie was caught off guard and nearly spilled his water. “Well, I do, Grandmere. I’m engaged!” he said with a smile.

“Who is she?” Aunt Antonia asked.

Eddie pointed to me. "This is my fiancée, Shelly Anderson."

"Her," Aunt Antonia said, disdainfully. She noticed me for the first time. "Eddie, you could have done better than that."

Eddie's face tensed in anger, but he didn't say anything.

"But she's not even a vampire!" Aunt Antonia said.

"Does it matter?" Eddie asked as he gripped my hand, not realizing how tightly he was holding it. But I dared not tell him.

Uncle Phillip nodded. "Vampires have certain privileges." He was still angry that I had questioned his company's production methods.

"Privileges! What do you mean by that?" Eddie snapped.

"Well, for one thing," Uncle Ludwig answered, "we vampires do not have to deal with the commoners unless they are serving us. Apparently, you have not learned that with your choice of a bride."

That last statement hurt me. Did this pompous, pig-headed Dracula look-alike think I was beneath him?

"Perhaps, she still has something of importance," he sneered. "What is your occupation?"

"A librarian," I replied.

"Hardly an important job!"

I crossed my arms over my chest. There was no way I was going to take any more of Uncle Ludwig's degrading insults. "Oh, and being an opera singer is more important?"

The entire table fell silent. Bianca looked at Rudolf. She liked me already. According to her, I was a feisty one. Uncle Ludwig got up from his seat and glared at me. "You have a lot of nerve insulting me. You are a worthless mortal who—."

He never finished his sentence because Eddie was out of his seat so fast I didn't even hear his chair move back. Anger flashed in his green eyes. "Don't you dare talk to Shelly like that," he said his voice dangerously low.

There was a flash of fear in Uncle Ludwig's arrogant eyes. Then he left the table in a big angry huff. Uncle Phillip and Aunt Antonia looked at each other in dismay. At least, they weren't speaking their malicious thoughts toward me.

"Well, at least I'm the responsible one in the family," Lukon said as he put his arm around Bunny.

Eddie and I shot a glance at each other and managed to

stifle down a snicker. Lukon's idea of responsibility didn't focus on dating someone who belonged to the world's oldest profession.

"That's nice, dear," Bianca said to Lukon, her voice dripping with sarcasm. Then she started asking me about my life and how Eddie and I met. She and Rudolf were sincerely interested in us.

Chapter Five:
Eddie Gives Me a Valuable Birthday Present

Before bed that night, Eddie walked me to my room. He held my hand. "I'm sorry about my family," he said.

"Your grandfather and grandmere are so sweet," I said.

He looked at me. "I meant Uncle Ludwig and the Duke and Duchess. I didn't expect them to be so rude and stupid."

"It's all right, Eddie. We just won't invite them to the wedding."

"Eddie!" someone shrieked from across the hall.

We both looked up to see a drop-dead gorgeous vampire come running up the stairs in a pair of black, three-inch stiletto heels. She was wearing a tight, leather micromini skirt and a bright red tube shirt. Her long, bleach-blond hair looked like she had used a can and a half of hairspray. Hello, the eighties are calling! They want their big hair back! She had pretty brown eyes, but her heavy makeup detracted from their beauty.

"Eddie, how are you?" she said, giving him a much too-long hug.

Eddie tried to push back from her. This was awkward for him. His not-so-subtle cousin was hitting on him. In front of his future wife, yours truly. "Ah, good!" he stammered. "How are you doing, Katya?"

She reached up and began to play with his hair before answering. "Much better now that you're here."

Eddie, I said, *get your cousin off of you. I'm the only one who's allowed to play with your hair.*

He pushed her away. "Katya, I would like you to meet my fiancée, Shelly," he said as he grabbed me and pulled me very close to him.

Katya laughed. "You're so funny, Eddie." She didn't believe him.

It was time for me to step in. "Yep, Eddie and I are getting married on September 18th. We just set the date on the ride over here."

Her jaw dropped. "But you promised your heart to me, Eddie." In her mind, she was replaying this fantasy of Eddie having told her they would become some kind of a couple.

"No, I didn't," Eddie said, cringing at the thought of them being together. His hand reached for my doorknob. "Well, good night!" he said hastily. Turning it quickly, he and I rushed in and slammed the door.

We both waited breathlessly until we heard the stiletto heels walk away from my door. Then Eddie breathed a huge sigh of relief. "That was awkward!"

I sat on the blue leather couch and crossed my arms. "You think? You failed to mention that cousin in your warnings on the train."

"I try to wipe Katya's sexual advances from my mind," he replied as he joined me.

"So, tell me about her," I said. I wasn't worried about Eddie being around her. He didn't even like her.

"She's a barista."

"And dresses like that?"

"She works at Buns."

"Oh." The franchise Buns (slogan: We have sweet hot buns) is the coffee shop version of Hooters. Just like the famous "wings" of Hooters, guys love to go to Buns for their "pastries."

"Your family's so dysfunctional. Lukon is a playboy, Katya hits on you, your Uncle Ludwig is a self-centered opera singer, and your Aunt Antonia and Uncle Phillip think they are the best thing since sliced bread."

"Not their blood company." Eddie smiled. "At least you got me." He looked around the room and noticed the book he gave me for my birthday. "I see you brought your present."

"Yeah, about that," I began. "Why did you give me that book?"

"Well, it's not just a book."

I looked at him as he retrieved it from my bed. When he placed it in my lap, I began flipping through it. "What do you mean?"

"Read the first line on the cover."

I closed the book and read the cover. "Knowledge is power." Suddenly, green sparks began swirling around the book.

We both watched as the book began to change its shape completely. A few seconds later I held a sword encased in a red leather sheath in my hands. I stood up and slowly pulled on the matching red leather hilt and out came a sharp, sixteen-inch silver blade. My eyes must have been as big as saucers. "Whoa! This is so cool!"

"It's for your protection."

"What?" I said.

"After the doll incident, I wanted to make sure you're always safe. I know you can take care of yourself, but this will help you. Plus, no one expects a sword to be pulled on them."

"Why a sword? Why not a gun?"

"Because you're a lousy shot."

"I killed that book demon with a vaporizer."

"A vaporizer is your basic, giant point-and-shoot weapon. A five-year-old can shoot a vaporizer."

I wondered who in their right mind would give a kindergartener a vaporizer. Eddie was right about my shooting abilities, though. Killing that book demon was a combination of my genius plan and a lot of luck.

"You're much better at hand-to-hand combat anyway."

I was a little bit hesitant about the sword. I had no idea how to use one, and I didn't want to cut myself. "How do I change it back to the book?" I asked as I put it back in the sheath.

"David said to use the second line on the cover."

I thought for a moment and then remembered. "Without Knowledge, there is no Power," I said. Green magical sparks reappeared as the sword changed back to an ordinary book. "So, David had a hand in this?" Eddie's trusted mentor, David Endora is a three-hundred-year-old wizard who doesn't look a day over fifty.

"Yeah, I told him I wanted to get you a weapon for protection. Have you ever heard of the Book Guardians?"

"No. Who were they?"

"They were a group of scholarly librarians back in medieval times. Back then the king of Zephyr wouldn't allow the peasants to read on their own."

"I take it this king didn't believe in freedom of speech."

"Looks like it. Anyway, the king wanted to burn all the

books and kill the librarians in the kingdom. So, the librarians decided to arm themselves by disguising their weapons in the form of books."

"So, this is one of them?"

"Kind of. What David had me do was take a piece of your DNA. I took some hair out of your comb the other day. David infused your hair with the pages of the book so that the book/sword only responds to your voice."

"This is neat, Eddie," I said. I wrapped my arms around the vampire's neck and kissed him. "I love it, but you're going to have to teach me how to swordfight."

"Unfortunately, I don't know that much about sword fighting. When we get back to Zephyr, David said he would teach you. In the meantime, read the book so you can get a feel for using the sword."

I smiled at him as I fingered the book. I couldn't believe Eddie had given me a book that could turn into a magical sword at my command. I now had the coolest concealed weapon in the world. I decided to start reading the book and practicing with the sword as soon as I could.

"Well, I guess I should be going to bed," Eddie said as he got up from the couch. He slowly opened the door and cautiously checked the hallway to see if Katya was still lurking about. He saw her and quickly slammed the door. "You know what? I think I'll leave another way." He swiftly walked to the sliding door leading to my balcony. Pushing back the curtain, he opened the door and stepped outside.

I followed him. The balcony overlooked a beautiful garden maze surrounding a huge fountain. "What are you doing?" I asked him.

"Well, to avoid my cousin, I'm going to have to get to my room another way."

"Aren't you worried about her getting into your room?"

He smiled as he pulled a key on a chain out of his pants pocket. "Not unless she knows how to pick a lock. I always keep my bedroom door locked whenever I come here." After slipping the key back into his pocket, he gave me a good night kiss before he slipped over the railing and jumped on the wall. Vampires can crawl up walls. I call it the "Spiderman effect."

I watched as Eddie quickly crawled along the wall over the

two sliding doors before he gracefully scaled the railing of his balcony. He waved good-bye before turning into a green mist and slipping under the door to his room.

Afterward, I went back inside, drew back the curtain, and went to fetch my pajamas out of my luggage. I began to unzip my dress. Remembering how awkward it was for me earlier, I immediately wished I had Eddie to unzip it for me. That opportunity would have to wait until our wedding night. After slipping out of the dress, I threw on my green and white striped nightshirt and matching drawstring pants and went into my bathroom. The robin's egg blue fixtures complimented the light pink guest towels laid out on the countertop. I wet the facecloth and washed the makeup off my face and then brushed my teeth. I grabbed the book off the couch and crawled into bed. It took only an hour to breeze through the short book before I shut off the lights and went to bed.

Chapter Six:
Never Bring an Angry Uncle
With You on Field Trips

The purple haze of dawn peered through the slits of the curtains. I could have stayed in bed, but I was supposed to meet Eddie and his grandparents downstairs in two hours. I grabbed some clothes out of my suitcase and took a quick shower. When I was done, I pulled on a purple sweater and a pair of nice-looking blue jeans. I slapped on some makeup and half-dried my hair before I put it in a French braid. I was sitting on my bed putting on my socks when I heard someone knocking on my door. I decided to grab my new camera.

"Shell, are you almost ready?"

"Just a minute, Eddie!" I said as I got up and unlocked the

door.

Eddie was wearing a long-sleeve red polo shirt with a white collar and a pair of black jeans. I was surprised to see him wearing a brand-new pair of shiny black loafers. He normally wears sneakers or boots, not loafers.

"What's up with the loafers?" I asked.

"Oh, these? Dirk convinced me to buy them."

"Are they comfortable?"

"Sure, I can see why Dirk wears them."

"You look good in them," I told him. I slipped into the new pair of brown ballet flats I bought last week.

Eddie looked me over with an approving smile but thought something was missing. "Why don't you wear your birthday necklace? It would go great with your sweater, babe."

"Okay," I said as I rummaged through my suitcase and pulled out the jewelry case. I took out the necklace and let Eddie put it on for me. I felt his cool fingers lift my hair and fasten the necklace's clasp. Once he was done, I turned around and he gave me an approving kiss.

"I like it," he said.

I locked my room before we headed downstairs. Bianca was waiting for us by the front door. She wore a charcoal gray business suit for the grand opening. Eddie and I felt a little underdressed. "Did you sleep well, Shelly?" Bianca asked.

"I did, thank you," I answered.

"I'm afraid Rudolf cannot join us. He has business to attend to."

Just then Ludwig came marching down the stairs. He was still in his full evening regalia, cape included. His clothes looked a little wrinkled, and when I mentioned it to Eddie later, he said Ludwig was a pure vampire. Slept in coffins and wore capes 24/7.

"I'm sorry I am late. Justine would not answer her phone." He began apologizing. "You're inviting her to the grand opening, Bianca?" He glared at me. "Tours are only for family members."

A flash of anger appeared in Bianca's eyes. "Shelly is going to be a member of my family. And may I remind you, Ludwig, you are only a friend of the family." She proved she was the matriarch of the family, and there was nothing conceited Ludwig could do about it.

We boarded Bianca's coach driven by Fritz. Bianca insisted I sat in front of her so she could ask me about my wedding attire. It was a lot of fun talking with Bianca about various weddings she had been to. Eddie, on the other hand, was forced to ride in silence with Ludwig.

When we arrived at the store, I was somewhat disappointed at how small it looked from the outside. It looked like your typical store with mannequins dressed in beautiful and very expensive-looking clothes in the display windows. There was a large, newly painted sign with the word Renfield's written in beautiful calligraphy. A small crowd of the undead gathered at the front door which had a huge red ribbon across it. Many of them were wondering why a mortal was here, but they figured I was just a tourist or an acquaintance of Bianca. When our small group arrived, someone handed Bianca a huge pair of golden scissors. She turned and addressed the crowd. "Welcome to the grand opening of the 100th Renfield's," she said eloquently. Then she cut the ribbon with great flourish and opened up the store.

When we walked inside, it was very elegant and much bigger. Rows upon rows of expensive designer clothes, both casual and business, hanging on clothing racks greeted us. Eddie and I could never afford most of these clothes, even with our paychecks combined. Bianca led us to the back of the store where the dresses were.

"Wow," I said as I took in the three rows of bride and bridesmaid dresses. The dresses were in every color imaginable and did not look like the typical, butt-ugly bridesmaid dresses. Instead, the dresses could be used for any formal occasion. I turned to Bianca. "May I take pictures of the dresses so Eddie and I can get an idea of what we want for the wedding party?" I asked.

She smiled at us. "Of course, you may, my dear."

I took my new camera out and began snapping pictures of the different dresses after instructing Eddie to hold them out for me. I wasn't going to try anything on but was doing a pattern search.

"Now, Shelly, you said your theme is going to be metallic blue," Bianca said.

"Yeah, the same color as the dress I wore last night."

"Oh, that is a pretty color. Once you find a design for the

bridesmaid dresses, let me know, and I will handle the rest of the details."

Both Eddie and I jerked up our heads in surprise. Yes, we couldn't afford the dresses, and we didn't want to impose on her kindness. "You don't have to," I said.

Ludwig who was looking very bored and very irritated spoke up. "Of course, she doesn't want your dresses, Bianca. She's too poor to want your charity. She doesn't realize how expensive fine clothes are. That necklace is very valuable, and she is not wearing it properly. In fact, it wouldn't surprise me if she stole it."

Not wearing it properly? I thought to myself. How many other ways are there to wear a necklace? And who was he to accuse me of stealing? "I am not a thief," I said pointedly. I secretly wished I could practice my sword-fighting skills right now.

Eddie clenched his fists in anger. "I gave it to Shelly as a gift."

Ludwig snorted in disbelief. "Really, Edgar, I should think you would have picked a better creature."

I think you should have picked a better sentence, Eddie thought. "Don't insult her, Uncle Ludwig," he said in a failing attempt to keep his voice steady.

"Oh, please, only royalty should be allowed to wear that kind of jewelry." He turned to Bianca. "I'm taking another coach home." With that, he stormed out of the store.

Bianca looked after him with anger in her eyes. "That stubborn pig! He thinks vampires should rule the world with an iron thumb. Some of us never change!"

"You shouldn't apologize for him, Grandmere," Eddie said. "He's just a friend of the family."

"Wow!" I said. "For a refined vampire, he's acting like a two-year-old who didn't get his way."

Bianca nodded in understanding. "I know. It seems like I have to though, or he will stop at nothing to get his way." She looked at me. "Despite what he said, Shelly, that necklace looks very lovely. Don't listen to a word Ludwig says. I swear sometimes I think he has no heart."

"I'll keep that in mind," I assured Bianca.

"Now, Shelly, what I was saying about the dresses is that

you don't have to worry about the cost of them. Think of it as my wedding gift to you and Edgar."

"Thank you," I said, surprised Bianca would want to make such a big contribution to the wedding.

Bianca smiled, her white fangs glistening in the glow of the fluorescent lights of the store. "Now, if you and Edgar would follow me, I will show you the rest of the store."

Chapter Seven:
Putting the "Fun" in Dysfunctional

When we got back to the mansion, I decided to put the necklace back in my suitcase. The last thing I wanted to do was set off Uncle Ludwig again. I was fresh out of witty comebacks. I changed into a little black dress with a matching dark red bolero and a pair of black flats for dinner.

Eddie met me at the end of the hall. He had changed into a black suit with a dark green silk shirt and black tie. We walked downstairs to the dining room. Uncle Konrad and Aunt Phoebe were already seated at the table, as were Dr. Karloff and Mr. Snerdly. Both of Aunt Phoebe's sisters and their husbands had already left. Lukon and Bunny were also gone, thankfully. Only Bianca, Rudolf, Uncle Ludwig, and of course, Kayta, remained.

Once Eddie and I sat down, Kayta eased into her seat which was a little too close to my fiancé, but I forced myself to be polite and only thought about stabbing her with a fork. As we ate another scrumptious meal of roasted potatoes, broiled broccoli smothered in cheddar cheese, and the best prime rib-eye steak I have ever had, Dr. Karloff began telling Bianca about his newest addition to his mobile autopsy unit. "I have made adjustments so it can travel over all types of terrain. This should make it easier for medical examiners in the mountains and the valleys where they don't have the equipment to move the unit properly."

I looked over at Eddie. "Robin mentioned the station just got one of the mobile autopsy units. The new medical examiner was very excited about getting it."

"Well, I only hope you put my name on the machine, Dr. Karloff, as I should receive full credit for it," Ludwig said, haughtily.

Dr. Karloff stared at him in anger. "You only gave me a piddling amount of funds for **my** invention. The only credit you received and will ever receive is that article in the medical journal."

Ludwig jumped up from his chair. "A footnote! My name was only in a lousy footnote!"

"You know what your problem is, Ludwig?" Dr. Karloff asked, his complexion turning from green to red. "You think the entire world revolves around you and you alone."

"Well, it should. I come from a long line of highly important vampires." He gave a great exasperated sigh. "If only I could reclaim the days when vampires were well-respected and not just a footnote."

Eddie shot me an Oh-Please look. *Here we go again. Uncle Ludwig is back on his martyrdom kick.*

At first, I was a bit dubious about his uncle's pity party. Then I was proved wrong as Ludwig began droning on and on about how it was back in the old days when vampires were treated with respect, how every vampire dressed befitting a vampire (such as in capes, suits, and the oh-so-dated widow's peak haircuts,) and how today's vampires (indirectly referring to Eddie) are changing and ruining the culture and traditions of vampires. At this point in the monologue, every vampire in the room was wishing the vampire slayers were back in business and driving stakes through their hearts so they would be spared the agony of having to listen to Ludwig drone on and on.

"Ah, okay, Ludwig," Bianca said awkwardly. "Thank you for that speech."

Ludwig got up from the table so fast he knocked over his glass. Dark red blood spilled all over the white tablecloth. "I can see I'm not appreciated." He glared as everyone exhaled a huge sigh of relief. "One of these days, you will remember what I said." With that, he turned on his heel and left the table.

There was an awkward silence until Dr. Karloff spoke to Rudolph and Bianca. "I don't understand why you still consider him a friend of the family, Rudolph."

"It's only because he was a close friend of Bianca's father," Rudolph said.

"I'm sorry that you have to deal with him, Bianca," Dr. Karloff answered with a sad shake of his head.

Bianca said nothing but pursed her lips together. If Ludwig kept up with his current attitude, then she would have to break her father's promise to keep Ludwig a part of the family.

I wondered if Ludwig had helped her out monetarily and was holding that over her head. I made a mental note to ask Eddie about it later.

We all finished our meal in silence. When the dishes were cleared off, the entire family began to migrate to the living room. Katya decided to corral Eddie and tried to make another attempt at hitting on him. "Oh, Eddie, darling! I'm getting bored. Let's escape away from here."

"I'm sorry, Katya," Eddie said as his eyes scanned for a quick escape route, "but I'm going to stay with my fiancée."

She was starting to slip her arm around Eddie's waist when I came in between and "accidentally" spilled my glass of red punch on her white shirt. "Oh, my gosh!" I gasped. "I'm so sorry!"

"Why, you little minx!" Katya shouted at me.

I gave her a shocked look. Who's being the minx? Who's hitting on my fiancé? "Look, I said I was sorry. It was an accident," I lied. I was getting fed up with Katya's antics. "Stop hitting on Eddie. He doesn't even like you."

"I suppose he likes you, a mortal?"

"Yeah! We're getting married."

She violently pushed me back a few steps. "You're wrong, you conniving Jezebel. Eddie loves me and me alone."

I could take her in a fight but decided against it. A catfight would not be in my best interest. I placed my hands on my hips. "What fantasy world are you living in?" I looked over at Eddie. *She's not listening to me*, I said telepathically. *Tell her the truth*.

Okay, Eddie said. He stepped in between us. "Look, Katya, I'm not interested in you. I never have been and never will."

His cousin's mouth gaped open in shock at his bluntness. "But we were destined to be together. I'm your true love."

"Sorry, Katya, but Shelly's my one true love. That'll never change."

Katya glared at him. "Uncle Ludwig was right. This mortal has ruined you." She stalked off.

Eddie looked at me. "Thanks."

"For what?" I asked.

"For mentally kicking me in gear to get rid of Katya."

"No problem."

"I thought she would take a hint."

"Not. Sometimes you have to be blunt to get your point across."

"Thanks for ruining me," he said with a grin. Suddenly, an idea came to him. "Come on, Shelly." He suddenly grabbed my arm. "I want to show you something."

I followed him up both flights of stairs. For the first time, I noticed an overhead trapdoor with a latch on the second hall's ceiling. He leaped up to pull it down. A long ladder came down and we climbed up to the musty, old attic. Eddie pulled the door shut behind us. "Come on, the surprise is on the roof," he said as he grabbed my hand. The attic looked like your typical attic, filled with boxes of junk, most likely from hundreds of years. There was a door to the right, and we opened it up to a widow's walk facing the back of the house. He hoisted himself over the railing and onto the shingles. Then he scrambled to the top of the roof. "Come on up."

I followed suit, careful not to slip and fall to my death. I grabbed Eddie's outstretched hand and sat down next to him. The aerial view of the garden maze and the fountain was even more amazing in the moonlight. There was a quaint small cottage attached to the end of the house. "Wow!" I said, breathlessly. "It's so quiet and peaceful."

Eddie nodded. "That's why I like being here. Away from everyone, including Katya."

"Can't imagine why," I said sarcastically. I held his hand and rested my head on his shoulder. "Who stays in that cottage?"

"That's Grandmere's studio where she works on all of her designs," Eddie explained.

"Oh." I said, "So, what do you do out here?"

"Sometimes I stay out here for hours. Gather my thoughts, and get away from the crowds. "Now I can be alone with you." That's what we did for over an hour. Sat on the roof taking in the majestic view in a comfortable silence, only passing a few sentences between us.

A chilly breeze blew past us. I hugged myself as I saw some storm clouds slowly gathering off in the distance. "Whoa, it's getting very chilly."

Eddie took off his suit coat and draped it over my

shoulders. "How's that, babe?" he asked me.

"A little warmer, but I'm still cold."

We went back inside to my room so I could throw on a sweater. When we walked inside, I was shocked to find my clothes strewed all over the floor. I picked up some of the golden dust sparkling all over the room and rubbed it between my fingers. I recognized it immediately. "Pixie dust!"

"What was Newton doing in here?" Eddie demanded.

"Your uncle must have let him in somehow."

"What for?" Eddie asked as he began to help me pick up my clothes and the book. "So he could find some proof you can't be a part of the family?"

"Or maybe, he's just a perv who likes to rifle through women's clothing." It took us a few minutes to put everything back in its proper place. That's when I realized the jewelry case was empty. The purple necklace was missing.

Eddie saw the box, too, and his face flushed with anger. "This is low, real low. He accuses you of being a thief and then has his employee do his dirty work for him."

We heard Jeffers calling for Eddie. He was knocking on

the vampire's bedroom door.

Eddie and I came out of my room. "What's up, Jeffers?" he asked.

Jeffers stopped knocking on the door. "Ah, Master Edgar, the family has called you for an important meeting in the living room."

"We'll be right there," Eddie said as we all started to head downstairs. He was having trouble keeping his voice steady, but I could sense the anger boiling inside him.

Jeffers shook his head. "I'm sorry, Miss Shelly, but Ludwig insisted only Mister Edgar attend the meeting."

"Did he now?" Eddie growled. He knew this whole thing was Ludwig's idea. He marched downstairs.

Jeffers looked down at me. "I'm sorry, Miss Shelly. The Baron believes vampires should only marry within their kind. He is a stubborn, pigheaded vampire who thinks everyone should heed his every word, not at all like Master Edgar. May I say something, Miss Shelly?"

I nodded. What was I going to do? Say no to the big man?

"Master Edgar is very happy with you. He truly loves you

and will stand up for you no matter what."

"Thank you, Jeffers," I replied. I liked the butler. Even though he was a quiet man, he was very observant.

That's when we heard angry voices coming from the living room.

"How dare you accuse me of stealing, Edgar?" Ludwig shouted.

"It's a matter of deduction. You're the only one with the pixie here, Ludwig!" Eddie snapped.

"The main reason for this meeting is to inform you the family does not want you to marry that mortal."

"The family doesn't want me marrying, or is it just you?"

"She is a peasant, a mortal, and not right for you."

I couldn't believe someone could say that. Tears of anger and hurt began to pool in my eyes, but I brushed them away. I wasn't going to cry.

"She has a name. May I inform you, that I am a grown man and do not have to get your approval for what I do with my life? I can marry whomever I please, and Shelly's the woman I will spend the rest of my life with, whether you like her or not."

"Ludwig, Edgar! Enough!" Bianca interrupted the argument. "Edgar, may I assume that Shelly's father approves of your marriage?"

"Yes, he does, Grandmere. I asked his blessing before I proposed to Shelly."

"Then I don't see what you're worrying about, Ludwig," Bianca replied.

"If I had it in my power, Edgar would never get the chance to bring this family to ruin," Ludwig said.

"Are you threatening my fiancée, Ludwig?" Eddie asked. "Because if you try to hurt her, it will be the last thing you ever do!"

I heard Eddie leave the room and met him at the head of the stairs. His muscles were very tense from the heated argument. We needed to talk in private, and I led him into my room. "Eddie?"

Eddie immediately noticed the angry tension on my face. He ran his fingers through his hair in an exasperated gesture. "I'm sorry you had to hear all that."

"It's okay," I said, my voice shaking with emotion.

"Don't believe anything Uncle Ludwig says about you," he told me as he held me close. "I don't care if you're mortal, immortal, rich, or poor. I love you, and that will never change, Shelly."

"I know. I just don't comprehend how someone could say those things."

"Uncle Ludwig is a heartless jerk, and there is no way I will ever let him hurt you."

I leaned my head against my fiancé's chest, feeling safe and secure in his arms. "You meant what you said about making sure that if he hurt me, it would be the last thing he ever did?"

"I did. I'm not going to kill him, but I might come very close. People can cut down my character, but nobody cuts you down. If Uncle Ludwig tries to hurt you, I want you to use your sword."

He was serious about using the sword for protection. I just nodded but said nothing. This would mean I would have to read the book a couple of times again if there was any chance of me using the sword to defend myself. I glanced over at my cell phone. "It's getting late. I should be getting to bed."

"Then I'll give you a kiss and let you get to bed." He tilted my chin up and gave me a long, passionate kiss. "Sleep tight, babe," he whispered in my ear.

"You, too, hon," I said. We parted ways, and I got ready for bed. Before falling asleep, I read the book twice.

Chapter Eight:
A Family Murder

It was a dark and stormy night. I know that's a cliché, but the thunder, lightning, and the hard rain woke me up. I fumbled for the light switch on my bedside lamp and pulled the chain. Nothing happened. We had lost power.

I looked out my balcony to see a reddish glow coming from somewhere outside. I was about to get out of bed when I heard muffled voices coming from the room right above me. Then there was some scuffling, followed by a horrific scream. I heard doors open on both floors and was about to grope my way to the door in the darkness. Suddenly, glass shattered and a bolt of lightning shot across the sky giving me a split-second view of a caped body plummetting past my window.

Then I heard pounding on my door. "Shelly, are you okay?" Eddie asked.

"Yeah, I'm fine," I said. I felt my way over to the door, and let out a yelp when my toe hit something hard. Finally, I limped my way over and opened the door.

Eddie was standing outside my door wearing only a pair of green and black plaid drawstring pants. He had two flashlights, both of which were shining directly into my eyes. "The power's out," he said, masking his concern about the scream.

"No joke, Sherlock," I said, snatching one of the flashlights from him. I bent down to rub my foot. "I stubbed my toe on something," I told him.

"Could it be that dresser drawer you left open?"

"Probably."

"Was that you screaming?"

I shook my head. "No, it came from the room above me."

Eddie looked up. "Uncle Ludwig's room."

"I heard some scuffling, a scream, glass breaking, and then I saw a body falling." I pointed towards the balcony.

Eddie walked over and opened the sliding door. The rain

beat down on the balcony as we stepped out. "Careful, babe," he warned me. "It's a little slick out here." He paused. "Wait, listen!" We leaned over the balcony and aimed our flashlights down towards the ground.

The family, Jeffers, Dr. Karloff, and Fritz were gathered around the crumpled and bloody body of Baron Ludwig Von Bela. He had impaled himself on the wooden fence that surrounded the edge of the garden maze. Despite popular belief, when vampires die again, their bodies don't turn to dust. Their bodies go through the same process everyone else does.

Newton was flying frantically about his master's body and darted up towards the balcony the moment he spotted us. "That's him!" he screamed in a high-pitched voice, pointing a tiny finger at Eddie. "He killed him! He pushed my defenseless employer off the balcony!"

The family looked up at us in speechless shock, thinking Eddie had killed Ludwig in a fit of anger. "That's a lie!" Eddie shouted at them. "I didn't kill him!" One of his hands began opening and closing as he prepared to throw a powerful energy spell at the pixie.

"Don't, Eddie," I hissed, pulling back his arm.

The pixie flew down to Bianca and Rudolf. "Have that man arrested! He killed my master!"

"Newton, calm yourself!" Rudolf ordered. "We'll have everything settled. Doctor, do you have your mobile unit autopsy unit with you?"

Dr. Karloff nodded. "I can set it up in my room, if you don't mind, Rudolf."

"Not at all."

"Mr. Snerdly!" Dr. Karloff called for his assistant. "Where the devil is he?"

A few minutes later, Mr. Snerdly shambled out of the darkness. He took one look at the impaled body, and a slow smile spread across his face. "At least someone had the guts to dispatch the scumbag."

"Enough, Mr. Snerdly. We will take your former employer, and the autopsy will tell us who did him in." Dr. Karloff and Mr. Snerdly slowly lifted Ludwig's body off the stake. Everybody watched as they lugged him inside.

Rudolf stood up to face us. "I want everyone inside the

living room, now! And that includes you, Edgar."

We walked back inside to my room. Eddie's hands were shaking with anger. "I didn't do it. I didn't kill him, Shelly."

I grabbed his hands. "I know you didn't, Eddie." This was not good. "Let's go downstairs and find out what happened."

A few minutes later, we were all seated in the living room. Everyone had changed out of their nightclothes and into their regular clothes. Candles and kerosene lamps cast dancing shadows across the walls. Uncle Konrad came up to Eddie. A look of concern was etched across his face. "What did you do, Eddie?" he asked his nephew.

"I didn't do anything, Uncle Konrad. You've got to believe me."

I glanced over at Eddie. I had never seen him this distressed before. Even though I knew for a fact he was innocent, as the daughter of a former police detective, I also knew he would be considered the prime suspect in a police investigation. I closed my eyes and concentrated on the minds of the vampires in the room. Someone here was guilty, and I was going to find out who and prove my fiancé's innocence.

Katya's mind was very clear. She was disgusted that Eddie could have killed Ludwig. How could she have ever loved a killer? She looked down at her newly painted nails and couldn't believe she had chipped them. She had no motive and was taken off my suspect list.

Uncle Konrad and Aunt Phoebe were talking quietly with Eddie. Uncle Konrad just could not believe Eddie would overreact like that and decided to call his lawyer once the power came back on. Aunt Phoebe was secretly glad Ludwig was dead so he couldn't harass her and her husband anymore about their own personal dietary choice. Like her husband, she was fearful Eddie would be in prison for a very long time. If it came to that, how was I going to handle everything?

Bianca and Rudolf were shaking their heads. They both were shocked Eddie could do something this drastic. At least Bianca wouldn't have to hear Ludwig's constant reminder that he helped her out monetarily when she started her business.

I had no chance to read Rudolf's thoughts because they were interrupted when Dr. Karloff enteredthe living room. He beckoned to both Rudolf and Bianca. Because the doctor was essentially made up of various body parts, I read his mind. Ludwig's death was a huge puzzlement to him. With that thought, he certainly didn't kill the vampire, or if he did, he was surprised at the results. According to the autopsy, Ludwig didn't die from a stake through the heart. He was already dead before he hit the ground. Someone or something had squeezed his heart to death without doing any outside damage to his body.

Eddie, I telepathically said, *I know how Ludwig died.*

He turned his head so fast I thought it was going to snap off. *How?* he asked mentally.

I told him telepathically. While I told him, the power came back on. I watched Jeffers blow out the candles and begin to put them away. The big butler had plenty of reasons to kill Ludwig. Treating him like a jerk was at the very top of the list. Bianca had Jeffers contact the police, but when he entered the living room, there was a solemn look on his face. "Mrs. Renfield, the bridge is out. The police won't be able to come until the bridge is repaired. It could take a day or so."

"Well," Rudolf said, clearly unsure of what to do, "I guess

everyone should go back to bed. Tomorrow, Konrad, the servants, and I will repair the bridge. Jeffers, I want you to make sure Ludwig's room is closed off until the police arrive."

As everyone shuffled back to bed, I grabbed Eddie's arm. "My room, now!"

Chapter Nine:
Eddie and I Disrupt a Crime Scene

Eddie looked at me strangely but didn't say anything until we arrived in my room. "What's going on?" he finally asked me.

"You think I'm not going to have a problem with you spending the next twenty-five to life in prison?" I said, placing my hands on my hips. "I know you're innocent, and I'm going to prove it to your family."

Eddie raised his eyebrow. "I appreciate your determination, babe, but how are you going do that?"

"By investigating the scene of the crime," I said.

"Isn't that illegal?" he asked.

"Not exactly. The police haven't arrived yet to call it a 'crime scene.' So, we're good."

Eddie shook his head at me. "Where is your moral compass?"

"I lost it a long time ago. Okay?" I began pacing around trying to figure out how to break into Ludwig's room without alerting the rest of the family. No doubt Jeffers had already put some kind of barricade in front of the door. An idea came to my brain on how to get into the bedroom. I grabbed my camera for photo evidence. It must have shown on my face because Eddie started following me onto the balcony where it had stopped raining.

"Shelly, what are you doing?" he asked.

I pointed to the balcony above us. "We can get in through that balcony."

Eddie looked at me dubiously.

"If you boost me up high enough, I can grab the railings and pull myself up. You can get up there on your own."

"Okay," he said, still not convinced at what I was doing but playing along. He bent down and made his hands into a makeshift step. "Ready?"

Throwing the camera over my shoulder, I stepped in and

grabbed his shoulders for support. "Okay, lift me up!" Up I went. My fingers barely brushed the railing posts. "I still can't reach them, Eddie."

"Get on my shoulders," he suggested.

"Okay." Stretching out my arms for some sort of balance, I managed to carefully climb on top of Eddie's strong shoulders. My boyfriend was grabbing my ankles so I wouldn't take a deadly topple like Ludwig. The balcony was still a little too high, and I had to jump to reach the railing. After I jumped, I realized I probably should have told Eddie what I was doing.

"Ow! You're crushing my shoulders."

I cringed. "Sorry. Okay, I'm going to try again." I felt the vampire tense his shoulders as I gave a little leap. This time I was able to grab the posts. It was then I realized that I have no upper arm strength.

Eddie let go of me and jumped up. He sailed past me, grabbed the top of the railing, and swung himself onto the balcony. Then he leaned over, ever so gracefully, and pulled me up.

"You're such a show-off," I told him, once we were on the

balcony.

"You know I only do it for you, Shelly."

I shook my head at him and surveyed the bloody glass shattered across the floor. "It looks like Ludwig came through here," I said. "Quite violently, I might add."

Eddie squatted down to inspect the glass. He took a look at the direction the glass had gone. It was completely angled. "I'm pretty sure he flew through the glass."

"Not of his own volition then?"

He nodded.

"Then any one of the other vampires here, Jeffers or Dr. Karloff could have thrown him out the window."

"Maybe, but why?"

"Oh, please. Everyone here had a very good motive, and don't forget an ideal opportunity." I paused in my ranting to glance over at the golden coffin-like box sitting in the middle of the room. "What's that?"

"I don't know. Want to take a look?"

We stepped carefully over the broken glass door and into the bedroom to inspect our find. The sides were covered with elaborate images similar to Egyptian hieroglyphics. The cover had more hieroglyphics with a raised engraving of your typical Egyptian pharaoh in all his glory, but right under it was the same star over a triangle just like the one on my necklace. I took out my camera and began to take pictures of the coffin. "It's a sarcophagus!"

Eddie was looking around the room for any clue as to who killed his uncle. "That doesn't surprise me. Uncle Ludwig was always buying different coffins to sleep in."

I had never seen the inside of a coffin much less an actual sarcophagus. "You wanna open it?"

"God, no! Why do you want to see the inside of someone's sleeping quarters?"

"What are you, chicken?" I challenged.

"Okay, someone's playing detective a little too seriously. Instead of opening the coffin, why don't we look for clues?" He glanced around until he spotted what looked like a piece of faded cloth snagged on one of the bed legs. It nearly crumbled in his hands when he picked it up. There were tiny black spots all over the fragile material.

"Is that mold?" I asked Eddie.

He shrugged. "I don't know."

"Smell it."

He shoved the cloth towards me. "You smell it."

"I'm not smelling it."

"Look, you're the expert on mold and mildew."

I snorted. "How do you figure that?"

"Who works in a library where people sometimes bring in books that are saturated in mold and mildew?"

"But who got the lovely opportunity to clean out behind the water heater at the diner last week?"

Eddie cringed at the memory. It had been an extremely slow night at the diner. Dad had volunteered Eddie to clean behind the water heater so the diner could pass this year's health inspection. "You remember that blue and yellow polo shirt you got me?"

"Yeah."

"I had to throw it away."

"Oh, gross!" I sighed. "We'll compromise, and we'll both smell it."

Eddie rolled his eyes but gave in. We took a whiff and looked at each other. "Mold," we said at the same time.

I looked around the immaculate room (aside from the broken glass). There was no sign of mold or mildew anywhere. I glanced back at the golden coffin and saw my necklace hanging over the side. I got down on my knees and grasped the necklace. It was stuck on something. "Give me a hand."

"What's up?"

"I found my necklace, but it's stuck on something inside the coffin. I need your brute strength to lift the lid."

Eddie got down beside me. It took him a few minutes to find something to hold on to. He grunted as he lifted the lid a few inches. "Hurry, Shell, this thing is heavy."

While snatching the necklace, I managed to take a peek inside the dark sarcophagus. "I think I saw something move in there! You wanna take a look?"

Eddie shook his head vigorously. "This thing is made out of granite and has a two-foot layer of solid gold on top," he replied as he set the lid down with a thud.

Suddenly we heard a tiny voice coming from the outside.

It was Newton. There was no way we could leave the room without the pixie spotting us. "Under the bed," I hissed.

We both scrambled under the bed just as Newton flew into the room. The pixie was muttering to himself. "I told him not to mess with the powers of King Runihura V. It was too dangerous, but the master wouldn't listen, and look what happened to him. At least, that weasel Edgar is being blamed for his death." He paused for a moment. "Well, maybe, I can kill two birds with one stone." We heard a tiny piece of paper rustle, and then the pixie began mumbling in what sounded like a foreign language. "Sus-lul-ee-pup u-nun-tut-i-lul yec-ou arur-e a-wuv-a-kam-e-nun."

I held back a gasp as the coffin began to glow a dark, hideous red for a few seconds before it fizzled out. We heard the pixie fly out of the room before Eddie rolled out from under the bed. *Stay here*, he told me. *I'll make sure he's gone for good.* He did a quick scan of the room before letting me know it was safe to come out.

"What just happened with the coffin?"

Eddie looked at it more closely before slowly backing

away. "Some type of weird black magic we shouldn't mess around with."

"I'm convinced. Let's get out of here." I said as I headed back to the balcony. As we peered over the railing, I realized something I had missed in my "plan." If we jumped, I would probably miss my balcony. Eddie might be able to carry me down on the wall, but I wasn't so sure if that would work. "So, any bright ideas on how to get down?"

Eddie smiled. "Easy as pie," he replied as he reached into his back pocket and pulled out a tiny black briefcase no bigger than the palm of his hand. Setting it on the ground, he said, "Maximum five!" The bag grew to normal size. Unzipping it, he searched through the wooden and silver throwing stars, the wooden stakes, throwing knives, and the two high-powered laser guns and ammo until he found what he was looking for—a long rope with a grappling hook at the end.

"When did you add that?"

"After the incident at the carnival," he replied. "Stand back," he warned as he began expertly twirling the hook and rope around. Then he heaved it at his target: the balcony on the widow's walk. After making sure it was secure and minimizing the bag, he looked over at me. "Climb on."

I climbed piggy-back style, and then he swung out over the ledge. I shut my eyes and held on tightly as he steadily climbed up the side of the building. Once we reached our destination, he easily swung both of us over the railing and onto the widow's walk.

I climbed down and looked towards my room. "Any particular reason why we didn't go down to my room?"

"Because I couldn't think of a safe way to get us both down. Plus, this way was much cooler." He released the grappling hook and put it back in the bag. "So, what's the plan, MacGyver?"

"We know Newton had something to do with Ludwig's death," I said as I followed him inside.

"So, how are we going to get him to talk? He's a pretty fast pixie." Eddie walked over to the trapdoor and pulled it open. He did a quick check to see if anyone was lurking about. "It looks like everyone has gone back to bed," he said in a whisper. He gently dropped the ladder and motioned for me to follow.

It took me only a few seconds to think of a perfect plan. "I have a plan, but we're going to need a few things from the kitchen."

Chapter Ten:
How to Trap a Pixie

There was nobody in the kitchen when Eddie and I arrived. This gave us an excellent opportunity to gather the materials for my evil plan. First, I found a medium-sized plate and handed it to my perplexed fiancé. "Care to enlighten me?" he finally asked. It was great to keep him in suspense for once.

"We're trapping a pixie!" I said as I opened various cupboards until I found an opened box of sugar cubes. I dumped four of them into a small serving bowl which I handed to Eddie. Then I opened the refrigerator and looked around until I spotted the next element. A bottle of maple syrup.

"So, when you lure him to your trap, how are you going keep him from flying away?"

By this time, I was opening a few drawers until I found the

last thing I needed to make my plan (insert evil chuckle here) complete. Grabbing a pair of kitchen scissors and the syrup, I turned to go. "Back to my room and I'll tell you everything."

Once we got back, I had Eddie set the bowl on the plate which I had generously drowned with the syrup. He was very impressed with my plan when I explained it to him. I slid open the door and set my trap on the balcony.

With scissors in my hand, I shut off the light and joined him by the door. The rain clouds had faded away, and the yellow moon gave us enough light to watch the trap.

We didn't have to wait long. Newton flew past us, whirled around, and made a beeline for the sugar. The scent of sugar and maple syrup was driving him crazy so he didn't even stop to check around the obvious trap. He landed in the maple syrup and began to savagely eat the first sugar cube he laid his beady eyes on.

Eddie and I looked at each other in disbelief. *He's a complete moron!* Eddie told me telepathically.

Like a lamb to the slaughter. Shall I?

I got up and opened the door. Eddie stayed hidden in the shadows and let me do the talking. Hiding the scissors behind my back, I approached the pixie. "You certainly like that sugar," I told him.

"You conniving harpy!" Newton snarled as he tried to fly away, but he couldn't lift off with the thick syrup all over his shoes. "Release me."

"I don't think so," I replied as I bent down and picked up the pixie by the waist with my left hand, leaving behind a long strand of syrup. "You're going to answer some questions. First, what were you doing in my room yesterday during dinner?"

"I'm not going to tell you anything," he spat as he struggled in my grip. Silver pixie dust flew off his wings. He tried to blast me with his sunlight ray, but the syrup on his hands was too thick and sticky.

This guy was feisty. I dangled him over the edge of the balcony. "Okay, I'll drop you."

"I'll just fly away the second you let go of me."

"Not with a clipped wing, you won't," I said, producing the sharp scissors.

He took one look at the huge scissors and shrieked in horror. "You wouldn't!"

I waved the scissors dangerously close to his dragonfly wings. "One little snip and you will be plummeting to the ground," I deadpanned with a completely straight face.

"Okay, I'll tell you everything. Master Ludwig had me steal your necklace from your room so he could complete the ritual."

That threw me for a loop. "What ritual?"

"The ritual for raising Runihura. But when my master did, something went wrong."

"What went wrong?"

"The master was killed!"

"By who?" I demanded.

"Him!" the pixie pointed a shaking finger up towards Ludwig's room.

I glanced up but saw no one. Something weird was going on, and it freaked the pixie out. He probably was going to have a heart attack at any time. "I'll let you go this time, but if you ever falsely accuse Eddie again," I paused dramatically and waved the scissors around, "Snip, snip! Got it?"

He nodded vigorously. "I'll make it even easier. You won't ever see me again."

I nodded as I released him. I watched him fly out of sight. When I went back inside, Eddie had turned on the lights and was now sitting on the couch, doubled over in laughter.

"Did you see the look on his face when you were waving the scissors around?" he asked in between gasps for air. "It was priceless!"

"Okay, am I supposed to be impressed you find my interrogation methods funny?" I asked with a smile. I got out my laptop and sat down beside him. I turned it on and listened to the motor hum as it warmed up.

Eddie grinned. "You would have been a great intelligence agent. What are you doing?" he asked as he saw me type the address of Findit.com, my favorite search engine.

"I'm going to search for that guy Ludwig tried to raise." Silently sounding out the way I thought the man's name was spelled, I began typing it in various ways. "Could you get me something to drink? This could take a while."

"Sure, do you want some water?"

I nodded without looking up from my computer. I heard Eddie leave the room. About fifteen minutes later, I found an article on King Runihura V. I jumped when I heard knocking at my door. "Eddie!" I called.

"Yeah, could you open the door for me? My hands are full."

I got up and opened the door. Eddie had a can of soda for himself, a bottle of water for me, and a bowl filled to the top with popcorn. Grabbing the water bottle, I opened it and took a much-needed drink. All of the planning with my evil schemes had left me very thirsty. "Thank you, honey."

"You're welcome, babe. Find anything?"

"I did. There's an interesting article on Findit.com."

We sat back on the couch, and Eddie looked over my shoulder at the computer screen. "What does it say?"

I shrugged. "Don't know. I was waiting for you. Want me to read it to you?" Balancing the computer on my lap, I stretched out my legs and rested them on my guy's lap.

"Why not?" he replied as he kicked off his shoes and put his feet up on the coffee table. He offered me popcorn which I took gratefully.

"'10,000 years ago in the desert kingdom of Nehebkau, the all-powerful pharaoh and sorcerer Runihara V reigned with an iron fist. He had been married six times, but killed five of his wives because they could not give him a firstborn son.'"

"Nice guy," Eddie commented. He popped another couple of popcorn pieces into his mouth before taking a sip of soda.

I smiled. His interruptions never bother me. Whenever I read something to him, he usually makes snarky observations. I continued. "'His sixth wife finally gave him a son, Runihara VI.'"

"Well, that was predictable. Did these people ever come up with original names?"

"When we have kids, we are not naming one of them 'Edgar.'"

"I would never saddle a child with that name."

"Glad we agree on that. Can I continue?" With his nod, I started up again. 'Soon after the birth of his son, Runihara V began to experience paranoia. Court scribes recount a time he saw his wife talking to a servant. Runihara V thought she was planning a coup. After he had her and the servant beheaded, he found out she was making plans for their son's birthday.'"

"Can we say 'paranoid?'"

"Oh, it gets better," I reached into the popcorn bowl and grabbed another handful. "'After that, he would torture and kill every person who even looked at him the wrong way. Runihara VI's nurse saw the destructive pattern his father was on and fled with the child to a safe house. When the child turned seventeen, he banded together with his father's enemies and led a swift and very successful coup.'"

"So, I'm guessing group therapy wasn't an option?"

"Get this. For his crimes, Runihara V was mummified alive and his sarcophagus was filled with flesh-eating spiders."

"That method seems a bit extreme. What about the old cut-off-the-head routine?"

"Oh, they tried that, along with burning him at the stake, stoning, drowning, running him through with a sword, and even poisoning him with a dose of arsenic strong enough to kill an elephant. Mummifying him alive and the flesh-eating spiders were the only ways to kill him."

"They wanted him dead."

"Ooh!" I said as I skimmed down through the rest of the article. "Here comes the curse. Before he died, Runihara V set a curse upon his tomb: Whoever disturbed his resting place will awaken him, and he will kill them."

"So, did this curse ever come true?"

"Yeah. A year later, his son opened up the tomb and died mysteriously. Many others who have been lured by the power and wealth of Runihara V have died under mysterious circumstances."

Eddie smacked his forehead with the palm of his hand and sighed. "Why couldn't Uncle Ludwig collect normal things, like stamps or baseball cards?"

A look of surprise washed over my face. "Your uncle collected coffins? That's really creepy."

He shrugged. "Supposedly he loved the feeling of sleeping in different places without leaving his mansion. He once told me he had ten coffins in his master bedroom."

"No wonder he was having marital problems." Then I thought back to the bitter conversation with Ludwig at the dinner table. "Eddie, you don't suppose Ludwig raised the mummy to help him take over the world?"

"Like an arch-villain, Shelly?" he asked dubiously.

I nodded. "Yeah, think about it. He always wanted to be in control of everything. Nobody ever did anything right, according to him. And what about his speech at dinner last night? Can we say, megalomaniac?" I shut down my computer and set it on the coffee table.

Eddie was silent for a bit, mulling over what I had just said. He took a handful of popcorn before answering. "This is not good. Not good at all. If he raised the mummy, then we've got to get rid of it before it kills someone else."

"How are we going to do that?" I asked him.

"We have to kill it when nobody else is in the house. I don't want any of my family getting hurt."

"Well, Katya is leaving early tomorrow morning, and everyone else going to fix the bridge. That will give us an opportunity to kill the mummy."

"That will work," Eddie said hesitantly.

I didn't like that hesitant tone in his voice. "Have you killed a mummy before?"

He shrugged. "No, but it can't be that hard. It's probably the same way one would kill a zombie."

"You have no idea, do you?"

"None whatsoever," he said. He leaned over and kissed me. "Don't worry about a thing, babe," he reassured me. "Let's sleep on it. I'm sure one of us will come up with a plan. Good night, Shell."

"Okay," I said with very little reassurance filling my heart. "Good night, Eddie," I said, and we kissed for a long time. After he left, I read the book one last time before going to bed. Tomorrow was going to be a big and quite possibly dangerous day.

Chapter Eleven:
Eddie and I Tick off an Evil Mummy

Instead of the sun waking me up, the alarm clock on my phone woke me up. The black digits on the neon green blared back at me:7:30 AM. I dragged myself out of bed, grabbed some clothes, and headed into the shower.

As I scrubbed the shampoo in my hair, I began to think about how Eddie and I could kill the mummy. Usually, when something was threatening our lives, I would always come up with a "crazy and dangerous, but ingenious plan," as Eddie put it. My fiancé always compares me to MacGyver.

Most of the time, my plans work. I racked my brain for any kind of plan, but all I had was a blank slate. Today MacGyver was no help whatsoever. I never saw a show where MacGyver had to dispatch a mummy. "Eddie better have a workable plan, 'cause I've got nothing," I said to myself.

Once I got ready for the day, I gathered up the empty popcorn bowl, the pixie trap, and the syrup and took it downstairs to the kitchen. Jeffers was there helping a plump vampire cook (Eddie had told me her name was Donna) with breakfast. They both looked at me holding the strange items in my hands. "Midnight snack," I lied as I handed over the melded mess of sugar cubes swimming in maple syrup to Donna.

She smiled at me. "Very good. Now, we have syrup for waffles."

I wavedgoodbyee to them and left the kitchen where I ran into Bianca. "Hi," I said.

"Ah, Shelly," Once again, the matriarch was elegantly dressed in some of her designer clothes. "I'm so glad I found you. I would like to show you something before breakfast."

I nodded, and we walked down the long hall in silence before I spoke up. "Eddie didn't do it," I said.

"I know how much you want to believe that, dear, but Edgar did overreact."

I wanted to tell her I could read the mind of every vampire here, but then what good would it do? She might say Eddie had planted the idea of his innocence in my mind.

"But don't worry, dear," Bianca assured me. "Ludwig had a very bad reputation around here. The courts may go easy on Edgar."

Great, I thought, *my fiancé may spend only a maximum of fifteen years in prison, instead of the usual twenty-five to life. Eddie had better come up with a plan to kill the mummy.*

Bianca finally stopped at a pair of huge double dark oak doors which she opened up. "If you wish, you may take a look at the books in my library."

When I stepped into the library, my jaw dropped. Tall cherry bookcases each with ten shelves lined the walls. Two green velvet high-back chairs with matching ottomans were next to a Tiffany floor lamp in the middle of the room. Two end tables were on either side of the chairs. A door leading to the garden was on the opposite side of us. It was even completely sound-proofed to send any serious reader into an uninterrupted Utopia.

I fell in love with this room filled to the brim with books. I gave a glance and noticed the books were arranged by subject and then by author. My eyes immediately found a large section on magical entities, such as the living dead, voodoo, and the like. Perhaps I could find a book on how to kill a mummy.

"You may stay here as long as you want. After breakfast, of course." Bianca said. But she said nothing about Eddie.

"What are you doing after breakfast?" I asked Bianca.

"I will be in my studio most of the day. I have to design some dresses for a deadline next week. Would you like to see my studio?"

The offer was tempting, but Eddie and I had a pressing problem on our hands. "Thank you for the offer, but I promised Eddie we would talk about the wedding." It wasn't a total lie. We would probably talk about the wedding if we survived the mummy encounter

Bianca smiled complacently at me. She was surprised that despite the "evidence" against Eddie, I was still going to marry him. What she didn't know was Ludwig's killer was sleeping in a sarcophagus two floors above us. "Perhaps another time then," she replied as we left the room.

Except for an occasional request to pass the food, breakfast was conducted with barely any conversation. The tension in the air was so thick it seemed almost impossible to breathe. Everyone seemed in a hurry to eat and run so they wouldn't have to hang around Eddie and me.

Bianca hurried to her office with Aunt Phoebe joining her while Rudolf, Uncle Konrad, Jeffers, and the rest of the servants left the house to repair the bridge. Which left Eddie and me all by ourselves in the huge house. We began to climb the huge staircase. "So," I asked him, "what's the plan?"

"Aside from opening the coffin, I have no idea," Eddie replied. "I was hoping you'd have a plan."

"Nope, I've got nothing."

"Not even a plan B?"

"Nothing."

"Okay, we'll improvise."

"Oh, good," I laughed weakly. "We're going to die."

"We're not going to die, Shelly."

"I don't know how to kill the mummy. You don't know how to kill the mummy. That leaves us with one conclusion: We're going to die."

"We'll figure it out. We always do."

"Yes, but we always have some semblance of a plan."

We arrived at Ludwig's bedroom door. Jeffers had done a good job of securely nailing in the piece of plywood, but that didn't stop Eddie. He had grabbed a crowbar from his grandfather's garage and began prying off the plywood. Once he was finished, he set the crowbar and plywood aside. One swift kick knocked the door open. "Ready?"

I slowly shook my head, gripping the book in my hand. I didn't feel even close to being ready toface offf with a deadly mummy. "Knowledge is power," I murmured. Green sparks ran up and down the book as it lengthened into the long, sharp sword. "Now, I'm ready," I replied, even though the sword shook in my hands.

We walked into the room. There was no sign of magic surrounding the coffin. Eddie confidentially walked over to the bed and took his briefcase out of his back pocket. When he started to use his spell to bring it to normal size, a black spark shot out from his hand. He snapped his hand back in shock. "Ow! That hurt!" he said.

"What happened?" I asked.

"I don't know. When I started the spell, a spark of magic just shot out of my hand." He furrowed his brow. "It must be some kind of countermagic spell." It took a few more sharp sparks of magic before Eddie was able to complete the spell. Upon opening the bag, he pulled out a pair of silver throwing-stars. "These should do the trick." He set the weapons on the bed and got down on his knees.

"Uh, Eddie?" I asked. "Are you sure this is safe? What about the curse?"

"Uncle Ludwig already cursed the tomb when he moved it here. Nothing is going to happen," he assured me. With a grunt, he pushed the lid off the coffin.

A mummy wrapped in old musty fabric lay inside the stone coffin. Its folded arms clutched a golden scepter. On its head, it wore a black and gold headdress similar to what King Tut might have worn.

The next few seconds went by so fast Eddie and I had no time to react. My fiancé was preparing to decapitate the mummy with his throwing stars when the stiff arms suddenly lifted holding the scepter in one hand. He mumbled something unintelligible just before a blast of black energy shot out from the tip of the scepter.

The sudden blast of magic knocked both of us backward. Eddie barely had time to release a force field spell to protect me but took the brunt of the blow. He slammed into the wall nearest the door.

Because the force field protected me from most of the mummy's spell, I just landed on my butt. The sword, however, flew out of my hands and went skittering past Eddie out into the hall. I was about to grab it when I saw the mummy leap out of the coffin. Eddie was slowly getting to his feet and didn't realize the mummy was coming straight at him. I ran over to my fiancé. "Move!" I told him. "It's coming towards us!"

He glanced up at the approaching danger and quickly got to his feet. "Go!" he urged me as we raced out of the room. He slammed the door. Grabbing a nearby chair, he jammed it under the doorknob to keep the mummy locked in

I grabbed my sword. "Without knowledge, there is no power," I said and it changed back into the book. Clutching the book to my chest, Eddie and I began running down the first flight of stairs.

"The article never mentioned a scepter, Shelly," Eddie informed me as we were about halfway down the stairs.

"Don't blame me, Eddie. It was an editable online encyclopedia."

A crash erupted above us and a chair-shaped object along with the bedroom door came sailing over us, barely missing our heads by inches. They landed only a few feet in front of the bottom stairs. Then we both saw the mummy leap over the balcony and land perfectly a few feet behind us. "Holy crap!" Eddie shouted, shocked at what just happened.

"For a guy who's been dead for ten thousand years, he certainly is spry," I said as we arrived at the bottom of the stairs.

Eddie grabbed my hand and pulled me into an open room. I pulled the door shut and started to lock it when he stopped me. "Shelly, I'm pretty sure a locked door isn't going to stop him." He flicked off the lights and we sank to the floor. Minutes slowly ticked by as we huddled together as far away from the door as physically possible. Finally, Eddie dared to get up and check it out. Stealthily, he crept towards the door before changing into mist and sliding under. A few terrifying seconds later, he came back. *He's gone*, he told me telepathically. *Let's go.*

We both peeked out the door. Not a soul was to be seen. After determining it was safe, we quietly made our way down the hall to the next flight of stairs.

"Where is he?" Eddie asked.

"How should I know?" I replied.

"I thought that you could read the minds of the dead."

I looked at him incredulously. "Eddie, the guy's brain was extracted piece by piece through his nose. Do you think the embalmer would have left one tiny bit of brain matter just so I could read his mind?"

"Well, someone's being a little touchy."

"We're being chased by a ticked-off mummy. I think I'm entitled to being a little touchy."

Eddie said nothing more as we quietly made it to the first

floor. The entire house was eerily still, but what made it even worse, was the fact the mummy was nowhere in sight. He might have used some kind of disappearing spell and could pop up at any moment.

"The library!" I whispered as a smidgen of an idea came to me.

"What? Why do you want to read books now?" Eddie asked.

"Your grandmere might have a book on mummies."

Eddie raised an eyebrow incredulously. "Why would she have something like that?"

"I don't know, but do you have a better idea?"

"No." It took him a few seconds to relent, but he finally did. "It's worth a shot!" He led the way, flattening himself as close to the wall as possible. *Stay behind me*, he said.

No worries there. I drew myself as close to Eddie as possible. We quietly passed the living room, the kitchen and the dining area without incident. When we arrived at the library, I set my book on one of the end tables and made a beeline for the section on magical entities as Eddie locked the door behind us.

My fingers swiftly flew across the spines of the books as I determined the topic of each one. Finally, I found an old red leather-bound book entitled *Sir Victor Bloodsmith's Guide to Defeating Living Mummies in the Heat of the Battle.* Dust flew off the edges of the pages and sent me into a sneezing fit as I began flipping through the book. First, I found the index and began to look for an easy way to kill a mummy. There was a loud POP!

"Shelly!" Eddie yelled. I looked up to see the mummy standing in the library. He held his golden scepter and mumbled another incoherent spell. A bolt of energy shot out at us, but Eddie intercepted it with one of his energy spells. "Hurry!" he shouted as he rolled out of the way of another spell.

I frantically turned to the correct page. "Got it!" I shouted. I skimmed down the page until I found my place. "Use your fire spell!"

Eddie nodded. He threw his palms forward. "Nebulae!" he shouted. Two powerful white fireballs escaped from his hands and sped toward the mummy.

But it was useless. The mummy turned the oncoming

fireballs into chunks of ice and sent them hurling back at us.

"Get down!" Eddie yelled. He leaped towards me as I threw myself to the floor next to him. "Any more brilliant ideas, Shell?"

"Try water," I said.

"I don't know a water spell."

I glanced up at the mummy coming towards us. "Use your fire spell right above his head. When he turns the fireballs into ice, throw two more just enough to make them melt. Then the water will drench him." I had no idea if this would work, but at this point, I was desperate enough to try anything.

"I'll give it a shot." Eddie scrambled to his feet and tossed up two large fireballs directly over the mummy. Just as I thought, he turned them into ice balls. Eddie then sent two more fireballs, ones with a little less power. The ice became watery and poured down upon the mummy.

The clothes and the brittle bones began to dissolve into a watery paste. Appearing out of nowhere, a black orb-like thing spun around the golden scepter that was lying on the ground until the scepter disintegrated. Then the black orb darted out under the library door.

"Well, that wasanti-climacticc."

Eddie was bent over, his hands on his knees.

"Anti-climatic?" he asked in between breaths for air. Whenever

he uses his spells in rapid secession, it always takes a lot out of

him. "We just killed a living mummy sorcerer with water! I would

say that was pretty climatic."

"Well, I just thought that it was going to be a little bit

harder. What was that thing that escaped from him?"

"What thing?"

"The black orb thingy. It went out the door."

"Oh, frig" Eddie's mouth formed a silent O. "Spirit

transfer!" He turned to face me. "Stay here." He headed towards

the door

"What's going on?" I asked him. "What's a spirit transfer?"

"It's when a spirit moves from one dead body to another."

He looked at me. "I want you to stay here. I'll put a magical ward

around the room where you'll be safe."

I shook my head. "I'm coming with you."

"No, you've never dealt with a spirit transfer before. It

could be very dangerous.”

I sighed. “I’ll stay. But if you’re not back in fifteen minutes, I’m coming after you.”

He gave me a long kiss. “I’ll be back sooner than that. I promise.” Then he left the library, closing the door behind him.

Chapter Twelve:
I Save Eddie and His Family

Waiting. It can be the most terrible thing. Especially when your fiancé is off to rid the world of an evil mummy's soul. Okay, not the world, but his grandparents' house.

Why didn't Eddie ask me to go with him? I wondered. *Does he think I would only get hurt, instead of helping him out? He always makes sure I'm safe in any dire situation. But I can defend myself with my sword. Perhaps he thinks I'm not ready for close combat. While he's out kicking some mummy butt, I'm going to practice sword fighting.*

I grabbed the book off the table and said the magic words. "Knowledge is power!" The green sparks flew around the book as it quickly changed into a long, sharp sword. I gripped the handle with both hands and jabbed the air. With what little practice I already had with the sword, it felt comfortable in my hands. I swung to the right, thrusting the sword with vigor. Then to the left. I dropped the sword and tried to catch it, but it clattered to the floor. That would do me no good if someone was attacking me. It took me a couple of times, but finally, I managed to catch it before it fell to the floor.

My training went on for a while, and I almost forgot what was going on. I looked up at the clock on the wall. Thirty minutes had passed since Eddie had left me alone in the library. Call it women's intuition, but something was wrong. Sliding the sword into its sheath, I attached it to my belt on the left side. Then I walked out the door, prepared to face whatever was going on.

The rest of the house was eerily quiet until I came to the living room. The unconscious body of Jeffers lay sprawled on the floor. My heart started racing as I bent down and felt for a pulse. Even though he was undead, I could feel a very faint pulse. At least he was still alive. I began to shake the butler on the shoulder. "Jeffers, Jeffers! Come on, get up!" But nothing happened. Someone or something incredibly strong must have knocked the big man out.

Stepping over his body, I tried to open the double doors of the living room. "Crap!" I said under my breath. They were locked. Pressing my ear against the wood, I could hear someone walking around and the labored sounds of someone trying to breathe. What was going on?

I wondered if I could just kick open the door as I had seen on television. Then I decided against it for two main reasons. One, I was not a cop nor will I ever be one, and two, I would probably trip over Jeffers. I looked around for something to break down the door. That's when I saw the heavy metal umbrella standing near the front door. Sprinting to the stand, I dumped the wet umbrellas onto the floor and picked up the stand with both hands. Staggering under the weight of the stand, I waddled over to the locked door. I got into position and rammed the base up and under the doorknob with all my strength. The doorknob buckled under the stress, and the lock sprang apart. Setting the stand down, I drew my sword and gave the door a good solid kick. It flew open and I stepped inside.

My mind did a quick analysis of the situation. Ludwig was up walking around with his back to me. *How could that be? He's dead*, I thought. Then I realized what had happened with the spirit transfer. The spirit had to enter a dead body. Hence, it chose the only one available: Ludwig. I decided to take a quick peek inside the vampire's mind. Or what was left of it which was nil. The spirit of the sorcerer pharaoh had taken over Ludwig's mind and body. It was like a scene from *Invasion of the Body Snatchers*, only without the aliens. He had the golden scepter in his hand and was using it to cast a spell to torture his victims internally.

His victims happened to be Eddie, Bianca, Rudolf, Uncle Konrad, and Aunt Phoebe. They were all clutching their heads as if they were about to explode. Fear gripped me for a moment until my inner voice screamed at me to do something.

"Hey, Moldy Pants! Leave my fiancé and his family alone!" I shouted as I gripped the handle of the sword.

Ludwig turned to me and stared at me with his blank, colorless eyes. "Duracell!" he shouted in a deep, gravelly voice that sounded as if it came from the bowels of Hell.

A stream of black energy shot from the tip of the scepter and headed straight for me. I instinctively swung the sword at the spell, thinking I could somehow repel it like a bat hitting a baseball. The spell hit the blade and ricocheted back towards Ludwig, knocking the scepter out of his hand.

I stole a glance at the sword. Nothing had happened to it. Would you look at that? It could deflect magic. I shoved that little bit of information to the back of my mind as I saw Ludwig running for the scepter. *He's useless without his scepter wand*, I realized. I got to the wand first and kicked it out into the hall.

"Thou will pay for that, wench!" he growled at me. Then he began to charge.

I stood in a fighter's stance, not knowing what to do. As he neared me, I closed my eyes tightly and swung the sword as hard as I could. A scream was cut off as the blade sliced through flesh and bone. I opened my eyes to see the severed head of the possessed vampire topple to the floor, followed by his body. The spirit shot upwards and burst like Fourth of July fireworks.

Eddie unsteadily got to his feet and came over to me. He gently pried the sword from my vise grip. "It's all right, Shelly," he whispered. "You broke the spell."

"I just killed him," I said in a very shaky voice. "I just killed someone." A very strong wave of nausea swept over me as I dropped to my hands and knees. "I think I'm going to throw up," I told Eddie, and I did.

The next day, Eddie and I were back on the train going home. Rudolf and Bianca decided not to press charges against Eddie but called off the rest of the reunion. They realized Ludwig had been killed while raising the mummy, but they decided to tell his estranged wife he had died from a fall off his bedroom balcony. Jeffers was doing fine. The only thing he had to deal with was a large bump on the head.

"I'm going to need a vacation from this vacation," I told Eddie as I leaned against him.

He clasped his hands behind his head and leaned back against the seat. "Tell me about it."

We hadn't had a chance to talk about what happened the day before. "So, what happened in the living room?"

"Well, I went out to find Grandmere and Grandfather and

realized the Ludwig—." He paused, struggling for the right word to describe his dead uncle.

"Pod person?" I suggested. "Like from the *Invasion of the Body Snatchers*."

He smiled at me. "Ludwig pod? I guess you could call it that. Anyway, he had herded my aunt and uncle and my grandparents into the living room after knocking out Jeffers. Once I was inside, the Ludwig pod started going on and on about how he was going to take over the world."

"Didn't he realize the whole 'take over the world thing' has never once succeeded, but has failed miserably every time?"

"Probably not. Then he hit us with this mind-blowing spell."

"Mind-blowing?"

"Our heads would have imploded within an hour." I shuddered involuntarily at the very thought, and Eddie put an arm around me. "And then you burst in, guns a' blazing!"

"More like swords a blazing," I said.

"Nice touch with the 'Moldy Pants' insult."

I still couldn't get over the fact that I had killed a man. "I can't believe I killed him."

"Shelly, he was going to kill you. I saw it. You did it out of self-defense."

"Then why do I feel so bad?"

Eddie lifted my chin so I could look into his face. "It shows that you have a conscience. You didn't want to kill him, but you had to make a choice: you or him. You made the right choice, babe. I'm proud of you. You put your life on the line to save me and my family. I'm glad I have you to watch my back."

"Me too." I leaned over and gave him a long, passionate kiss.

COMING SOON

Election of the Undead

My Life Among the Undead:

Book Seven

By
Camara M. Bragdon

When Zephyr's mayor is vaporized by a strange creature at a baseball game, two members of very different political parties start competing for the newly opened office. Shelly Anderson and Eddie Van Helsing unwillingly find themselves thrown into a game of political mystery and intrigue after Eddie's mentor, David Endora, is accused of using black magic and murder. As they dig deeper, Shelly and Eddie discover many secrets, some worth killing for. Can the telepathic librarian and the vegetarian vampire solve this mystery before time runs out for David?

ABOUT THE AUTHOR

Camara Bragdon has her master's degree in library and information science and lives in Maine. This is the sixth book in her vampire series, *My Life Among the Undead*. Visit her website at www.camarambragdonauthor.com

www.ingramcontent.com/pod-product-compliance
Lightning Source LLC
Chambersburg PA
CBHW040827010826
48978CB00012BB/636